I0535131

Goats, Apples and Conspiracy

Apple Creek R-Parks Department Mysteries

Montie Red

COPYRIGHT © 2025 MONTIE RED

ISBN: 978-1-962293-12-9

Cover design: MRed

Map Illustrator: M Red

Library of Congress

 Formatted with Vellum

To my biggest and most interesting mystery in life, Josephine

creek

Ice Cream&Flower Shop

Chapter 1

"Long ago, a young woman named Ruth lived right here on this farm," said the volunteer girl sitting on an old couch in the middle of the farmhouse's living room. "Ruth had four goats she loved very much. Their names were Spring, Summer, Autumn, and Winter. Can you guess why?"

The children sitting cross-legged on the floor lit up. Although a few raised their hands, most of them just shouted, "Seasons!"

"That's right—she named them after the seasons!" The volunteer lowered her tone as she leaned forward and continued. "Ruth and her goats were the best of friends. They followed her everywhere—through the fields, to the barn, even to the garden. The neighbors used to say you could always hear them coming, because Ruth would laugh and the goats would bleat right back."

"Not exactly how I remember this one," my sister Sandie whispered in my ear.

I nodded, hoping this sweet volunteer had a gentler ending than the version we'd grown up with.

"One evening," the volunteer went on somberly, "Ruth went out to check on the farm, but she never came back."

A few children gasped. Others turned toward their teacher, whose expression was as skeptical as Sandie's—and probably mine.

"What happened?" a little boy in the front asked.

"Did she die?" another one shouted from the back.

My sweet Darcy, now a proud kindergartner, shook her head. "How would they know if she died if no one saw her again? It's clearly a missing person's case, right?"

Sandie elbowed me as I tried hard not to laugh at Darcy's observation. Clearly, my daughter had spent too much time around police talk lately.

"Well, I don't know if it was a missing-person case," the volunteer said, reclaiming her audience's attention. "People searched and searched, but they couldn't find her." Before more questions could fly, she lifted her hand dramatically toward the back of the room. "Some say she moved far away to start a new adventure. Others imagine she became part of the land—and that her goats still watch over the farmhouse for her."

Her voice softened, and the little ones in front of her fell silent.

"Here's the fun part: visitors say if you listen carefully at night, you can sometimes hear the goats bleating near the farmhouse door. Maybe they're calling to Ruth, or maybe they're just saying hello to the people who come to visit. Either way, if you hear goats on a moonlit night, don't be scared—" she paused just a bit too long for dramatic effect, "you're probably hearing our new friends: Peach, Plum, Nectarine, and Bo—the goats that live here now. Who wants to feed them?"

With that, story time exploded into chaos. Darcy's teacher and the chaperones—myself included—tried to herd the excited group toward the barn.

As we walked out, a little hand slipped into mine.

"Mom, this was the best field trip ever!"

I made a mental note to thank Linda, our

R-Parks secretary, for the suggestion. It had been her idea to bring Darcy's class to Deaport Farm, the city's historical site, as part of the new educational program.

"I'm glad you're enjoying it," I said.

Darcy looked down and slowed her steps a bit. "I just wish Bruno could be here. He would love it!"

Before I could answer, a tall woman in a suit walking past the volunteers spoke from behind us.

"Who's Bruno?"

"Our dog," Darcy said proudly. "He's the best police officer—well, Ben and Logan aren't too bad either."

"That explains the police reference," the volunteer said with a gentle smile that made her look wiser than her teenage years.

The tall woman chuckled. "I wish my dog could come too, but the goats aren't very fond of dogs—and Walter would have a heart attack."

"Who's Walter?" Darcy asked.

"The old grouchy guy who keeps the history of the farm ongoing," the woman said. Then she turned to me. "Which reminds me— do you mind if I borrow your mom for a second, sweetie? Park stuff."

Darcy shrugged and gave me a quick hug before bouncing toward Sandie, who was outside the barn holding baby Leslie—now almost two months old—in her arms.

"I'm sorry to bother you," the woman said, lowering her voice. "You're Margaret Willow, right?"

I nodded, intrigued. "Do we know each other?"

"I work the front desk here some days," she said. "When I saw the registration forms for today's field trip, the name 'Willow' jumped out. It's not a common one around here."

I smiled, waiting for her to continue.

"My name is Thelma Jacobson, but my great-grandmother's was Deaport. This farm used to belong to my family." She hesitated, glancing toward the volunteer who gave her an encouraging nod. "I'm concerned about the future of this place. Is there a way we could talk privately?"

A knot formed in my stomach. Maybe it was her secrecy—or how easily she'd tracked me down. Although, my contact information was literally printed on the farm's pamphlets, right by the front door. Regardless of my gut feeling, I couldn't ignore a concerned citizen.

"Of course," I said, sounding more confident than I felt. "We can meet at City Hall—"

"No!" Thelma's voice jumped in volume, and she shook her head sharply. "Not City Hall. I don't trust it. Could we meet somewhere else?"

"Not here," the girl volunteer whispered, her hands trembling. "Please—it's important."

Suddenly, the warm, golden fall afternoon felt a bit colder. "What about Cyder's Pub?" I offered. "It's noisy but private enough."

"Yes," Thelma said quickly, relief washing over her features. "That would be perfect. Tonight, if you can? I know you're busy, but it's important."

The moment I nodded, both women visibly relaxed.

"Thank you," Thelma said. "We won't take more of your time. Every moment with your child is a treasure I wouldn't dare steal."

They turned and left me standing there, wondering what on earth had just happened—and why I hadn't paid more attention when the volunteer introduced herself earlier.

As Darcy waved at the goats outside the barn, I couldn't help but think how much Bruno would have loved sniffing around here

—though knowing him, he would've tried to herd them all into a single pen.

Darcy went back to school for another couple of hours, so after driving Sandie and baby Leslie home, I made my way to the office. Thankfully, Linda didn't have a pile of papers waiting for me. Since we had just presented the budget, I finally had time to focus on the fall festival—a supposedly simple task, because it was a city collaboration.

Or so I thought.

As if on cue, my phone rang.

"Margaret," a deep voice said. "This is Francis Terrance, the Parks Director in Maple Hollow?"

"Of course, Francis," I replied, following his friendly tone although we'd only exchanged a few emails before now. "I was just about to check the last details for the festival."

"Well, you may want to hold off on that," Francis said. The way his voice dropped told me the rest of my day—maybe my week—was about to spiral. "We have a situation here, and..." he sighed. "Maple Hollow won't be part of the fall festival this year."

I sank into my chair, bracing for impact. "What do you mean Maple Hollow won't be part of the festival? The festival *is at* Maple Hollow's orchard. Are you donating me your land?"

Francis chuckled, which only made my stomach drop further. "I love your humor, Margaret. No, I'm not donating anything, but you're right—we *used* to host the festival. A personal favorite, by the way. I was looking forward to working with you. But this year..." I heard papers shuffle on the other end before his voice lowered. "This stays between us for now —it's not official yet, but believe me, it's happening. We have a new mayor with big ideas, and the first one is to rename our city."

"A new *what*?" I said, blinking. Renaming a city wasn't something that happened every day. I'd had my share of mayoral headaches, but this was a new one.

"Mayor—and apparently, a new name," Francis said, frustration lacing his tone. "The whole thing's ridiculous. But you know how politics and historians get—especially when one's a fan of the other. The short version? Our city changed its name centuries ago, back when witchcraft panic was a thing. Anything that *sounded* magical was banished."

I didn't say it out loud, but "Hollow" sounded like something straight out of a Puritan sermon from the 1600s. "So, you're going back to the original name?" I guessed.

"That's the idea," Francis said. "But it's stirring up a storm in the council. The problem is, the orchard is where all that old history began. The farm was supposedly owned by a witch—or someone accused of being one."

"Do you have a missing person and goats too?" I asked before I could stop myself.

"What?" Francis sounded startled, then let out a small laugh. "No goats. Just a bunch of protestors with mixed opinions. Honestly, I'm afraid hosting a festival there would be a magnet for mischief and political nonsense."

The last thing I wanted was to wade into politics—but this was far from ideal. "So you're canceling everything?"

"That's up to you, Margaret," he said. "The vendors and residents love the festival. If you can find a new location, I'll happily send them your way—along with our stands and supplies."

"So I just need to find a place big enough to host a festival the size of our Arts Festival," I muttered, "in less than three weeks."

Francis gasped. "Oh no, you'll need it sooner than that—two weeks at most. I wanted to warn you early so you'd have a fighting chance. But if this isn't settled fast, the council will use it as leverage."

I groaned. "I really don't like politics."

"Isn't your town name Apple Creek?" Francis asked, half teasing. "You must have a couple of orchards over there, no?"

"You would think so, but," I said, "we got the name from the river that runs through town—it used to border a line of apple farms, back before they all stopped at your town's edge. The only orchard left here is a tiny setup for fall photos. But hey, we have plenty of maples if you need syrup."

Francis laughed. "I'll keep that in mind."

"Thanks for the heads-up," I said sincerely. "I appreciate it."

"Good luck, Margaret—and please, let me know as soon as you decide about the festival."

When the call ended, I stared at my desk, trying to summon a miracle. I could already hear my mayor's voice ringing in my ears, complaining about disappointed residents and lost vendor revenue. And Catherine Roberts, the councilman's wife, would have plenty to say—especially since she'd nearly taken over the Arts Festival last month.

I leaned back, glancing toward the empty spot under my desk where Bruno usually slept. The office felt strangely quiet without the soft rhythm of his breathing.

"Would've been nice to have you here today, buddy," I murmured. "But I guess solving crimes with Logan beats watching me panic over festivals."

I smiled at the thought of him—ears up, tail wagging, nose to the ground—probably more focused than half the detectives in the department.

"I was about to get going—are you all right?" Linda's voice came from the doorway.

I looked up, pushing a hand through my hair. "We have a major problem, Linda. Can we schedule a department meeting?"

"Of course," she said, glancing at the clock. "But it'll have to be tomorrow. We've got a council meeting starting any minute."

I groaned but gathered a few folders. The last thing I needed was to answer questions about a festival that might not even happen—and I couldn't explain why. Francis had made it clear the situation wasn't public yet, and I wasn't about to betray his trust. After all, if I somehow saved the festival, we'll need their vendors and supplies.

Chapter 2

The meeting wasn't as bad as I expected. Thank goodness our lovely city council had plenty of opinions about the bridge reconstruction, which meant they ignored the R-Parks Department until the last five minutes. I used that time to report on how well the new *Education at the Farm* program was going, and how nicely the animals—especially the goats—were adjusting to the visitors.

I almost forgot I'd promised Thelma and the mysterious volunteer that I'd meet them at the pub. So, I called Logan and asked if he could bring Bruno along. I wasn't sure how he'd feel about the change of plans, but he didn't seem upset—or at least I wanted to believe that. Over the past weeks, we hadn't seen much of each other, something I tried not to think too hard about.

Cyder's Pub was buzzing as usual, warm light glowing against the dark wood, and the scent of baked pretzels and cider filling the air. Mr. Elliot, the owner, spotted me from behind the bar and waved.

"Maggie! So nice to see you. Dare I hope your mom sent you?"

I chuckled—it wasn't a bad guess. My mom was one of his most loyal patrons. "Not this time. I'm meeting with—"

Across the room, I spotted Thelma. Thanks to her height, she stood out, even seated. From this distance, I could tell she wasn't comfortable—her eyes darted around the room as if she were expecting someone to leap out of the shadows.

Mr. Elliot followed my gaze and leaned in, lowering his voice. "Those two are a strange pair. Who manages to look that nervous in *this* place? Why don't you take the far booth by the window? Maybe the view will calm them down."

I smiled. Cyder's Pub felt like home to me —cozy, friendly, and always a little too loud for secrets.

"Thelma!" I called once I was close enough.

Her shoulders visibly relaxed when she saw me. Grabbing the girl beside her, she hurried over. "Thank goodness you're here! I hope we can find a table where no one can listen."

I wanted to reassure her that in this pub no one cared about anyone else's business, but I just motioned them toward the far booth. It seemed to satisfy them, though their wary glances didn't stop.

"I'm sorry," I said to the girl beside Thelma. "You mentioned your name during the presentation, but I can't quite remember it."

A shy smile brightened her face, softening her teenage features. She couldn't have been more than seventeen.

"Rose," she said quietly. "Rose Jacobson."

"So Thelma is your—"

"I'm her aunt," Thelma interrupted, her tone heavy with fact rather than affection. "Rose lost her parents when she was just a baby."

Rose's gaze dropped to her lap, fingers twisting together. It wasn't that Thelma was unkind—it was just the blunt way she spoke.

"I'm sorry for your loss," I said softly. Rose's smile in return was small but sincere.

Thelma cleared her throat and glanced

around the room again. "I just hope this is a safe place to talk."

A flicker of unease ran through me. Maybe I should have waited for Logan and Bruno to arrive before starting.

"We won't take much of your time," Thelma said, leaning closer. Her voice dropped to a whisper. "The last time I spoke to someone about this was with the city Historian Mr. Gray, and... well, he didn't appreciate our concern and almost threatened us."

A cold shiver ran down my spine. I definitely *should* have waited for Logan and Bruno.

"Are you familiar with the legend I told the kids today?" Rose asked, her voice barely above a whisper.

"Yes," I said. "And I think you did a great job making it kid-friendly. That wasn't exactly the version I grew up with."

Thelma exhaled in relief. "Good. Walter Gray pretended not to know anything about it. Have you met Mr. Gray?"

"I can't say I've met him in person, but I've heard of him."

Thelma nodded, but it was Rose who continued. "He ignored the warning, and now things are upside down."

I frowned. From what I knew, Walter Gray was a respected fixture in town—beloved by the council and practically part of the furniture at the senior center. "Is Mr. Gray against the educational program?"

"Oh no!" Thelma exclaimed. "He's in love with it! The more people at the farm, the better. That isn't the problem."

I opened my mouth to ask what the problem was, but Rose beat me to it. "It's the curse."

The word hung in the air for a heartbeat before Thelma gasped. She grabbed the salt shaker, poured a pinch into her palm, and tossed it over her shoulder.

"Rose! You can't *say* it like that! It'll make it worse!" She turned to me, pale and wide-eyed. "The legend is real, Margaret—and worse, it's affecting our town."

Her tone was so serious I couldn't laugh, even if I'd wanted to.

"You see," Thelma said quickly, "Walter's been trying to restore the farm to its glory days." She made air quotes with both hands. "He's been planning it for years, but now he's rushing things. Maybe he thinks he's running out of time, I don't know. But he didn't ask anyone's opinion."

I leaned forward. "And that's a problem because...?"

"He dared to bring goats to the barn!" she declared, voice rising. "Goats! Do you know what that means?"

I shook my head carefully, half-expecting her to hex me for not knowing.

"Ruth used to own goats," Rose explained in a steady, matter-of-fact tone.

"So you think the new goats are—"

"Those animals are cursed. The legend is very clear!" Thelma interrupted, slapping the table so hard the glasses rattled. "The goats are looking for Ruth. Mischief will keep happening until they find her."

"Mischief will keep—"

"Don't pretend you haven't noticed it, Margaret," Thelma cut me off, her voice trembling. "The council chaos, the delays, the constant interruptions—the murders. How do you explain all that? In just a few months? It's the goats."

Her words painted a chilling picture. I thought of the strange call from Maple Hollow earlier that day.

"The goats have to go," Rose said softly, her voice slipping into that same story time rhythm she'd used with the kids. "We shouldn't play with tragedies from the past. Ruth can't be alive, but the goats won't stop—not until they get what they want."

She shook her head while Thelma sat back, wringing her hands. "They can't help it, Margaret. Ruth's disappearance binds them. The curse will stay until that case is solved—and we both know century-old crimes don't get solved in real life."

Even with the pub's chatter and laughter around us, I felt an eerie hush settle over our booth. Then, something brushed against my hand—warm and familiar.

"Bruno!" I gasped as his big head appeared beside me. He jumped onto the bench and gave my cheek a sloppy lick. "Hey! I missed you too, but you nearly scared the life out of me!"

Logan cleared his throat from behind us. "Sorry, didn't mean to interrupt."

"We're leaving," Thelma said suddenly, pulling Rose to her feet. "Just remember, Margaret—the goats have to go."

Rose gave me and Logan a small, apologetic smile before following her aunt out of the pub.

Logan slid into the booth across from me, glancing at the door they'd just exited. "That sounded serious," he said, snagging a napkin. "Anything I should know?"

Bruno huffed softly under the table, resting his head on my knee. I scratched behind his ears, grateful for his steady presence—and for once, didn't have a single clue where to begin.

"Goats?" Logan asked when I got to that part of the story. He popped a fry into his mouth, one eyebrow raised. "That's not the legend I remember. Or is it?"

I shrugged. "I'm not sure. Unlike you, I never went to the barn at night."

He placed a hand over his chest, all mock innocence. "I would never do such a thing, Miss Willow."

Leaning across the table, I smirked. "Mr. Forest, I know very well you did. More than once. You and Henry Klauer picked up my sister from my house after curfew—don't deny it." I stole a fry from his plate.

"Hey, stealing is illegal," he said, pointing at me with his remaining fry, "and so is having that good of a memory."

I sighed, leaning back against the booth.

"This is crazy, Logan. How exactly does one go about fixing a curse?"

Logan cleared his throat, but instead of laughing, he humored me. "Well, I suppose the goats need to find Ruth. I can't remember all the details, but we used to walk to the barn, turn our backs to it, and wait to see if we heard them bleating. Supposedly, if you stood perfectly still, they'd cry—and then they'd show you where Ruth was."

I frowned and crossed my arms. "I thought if you heard them, it meant they'd *take* you to Ruth. As in... permanently."

He tilted his head, palms up. "Tomato, tomahto. Either way, you'd find her."

I shook my head. "I'd rather not find her at all. Hasn't she been missing for, oh, a century or so?"

"I guess so." He paused, thoughtful. "Which raises the real question—how are these *the same* goats?"

He had a point. A silly one, but still. Thelma and Rose had already hinted at it. "According to Thelma, the curse affects all goats."

"All goats? How didn't it happen until now?"

"Walter Gray was the one who insisted on

bringing goats back to the farm—for the first time since Ruth's disappearance."

"Walter Gray?" Logan's mouth curved into a grin. "He used to be my history teacher. Speaking of century-old things."

"Logan!" I scolded. "He's fine. Still our city historian and all."

He chuckled, reaching for another fry. "That says a lot about this town. We've got a ghost and goats running it."

I rolled my eyes and mimicked his laugh, then asked, "So how do you explain the murders, the missing paintings, all the festival chaos? And now Maple Hollow on top of it?"

"That," Logan said, wiping his hands with a napkin, "would be Maple Hollow's problem, Maggie."

I shook my head. "Maybe I shouldn't have told you about that. It's a secret."

His expression softened. "All right, Maggie, listen. First of all, you can always trust me. I won't say a word about that other city or their problems. You know that, right?"

I nodded, but he didn't give me the chance to speak.

"And second," he went on, "to many—Apple Creek might be peaceful, but there's still crime here. Otherwise, I wouldn't have a job."

"So, you don't think any of the recent events have been... extra strange?"

He grinned, his smile bright enough to make me forget the question. "Well, you're back in town. That's a wonderfully strange event in itself."

I hadn't expected that. My cheeks warmed, and I looked away before he noticed. Still, the question that had been tugging at me for weeks finally slipped out. "If that's so, how come I haven't seen you much since the wedding?"

"Lucy's wedding?" he asked, his voice cautious.

"Yes, *that* wedding."

He exhaled and ran a hand through his hair. "It wasn't the wedding that changed things, Maggie." His tone softened. "Ben mentioned how chaotic things are at your house. With Sandie being there more than usual, and baby Leslie keeping everyone up—you're right, I've been distant. But I thought you needed the space. I didn't want to add to the exhaustion."

I blinked a few times before laughing. "Poor Ben. This must be his first grandbaby."

Logan's shoulders relaxed. "So... I can visit, then?"

I tilted my head, pretending to think. "Well, Ben might be right—the house is chaos.

Sandie and Leslie have opposite sleep schedules. But if you call, I'll have a great excuse to escape. Toby and Darcy are probably tired of the park by now anyway."

"Noted," he said with a grin. Somehow, the butterflies in my stomach decided to host their own festival.

To distract myself, I changed the subject. "What am I going to do? Where am I supposed to move those goats?"

Logan reached across the table and took my hands, his touch warm and steady. "Maggie, are you also sleep-deprived?"

"Excuse me?"

He laughed softly. "You don't need to *fix* a curse. Listen to yourself. What you need is to find a new location for the festival. That's your only real problem. Let those women handle their superstitions—don't get caught up in it."

As his words sank in, the world felt a little lighter. "You're right. The goats have their home at the farm, and I just need to find a place for the festival—not to break some old curse."

Logan leaned closer, voice gentle. "And maybe take a nap now and then. Or move to Sandie's for a few weeks."

I frowned, but he only winked.

Beneath the table, Bruno let out a low,

sleepy sigh, as if agreeing with Logan. He'd been curled up at my feet the entire time, occasionally thumping his tail whenever Logan's voice grew softer. I reached down and rubbed his back.

"You hear that, Bruno?" I said. "Your partner thinks I need a nap."

Bruno gave a quiet huff—half protest, half agreement—and settled again.

"Smart dog," Logan said with a grin.

I rolled my eyes but smiled all the same. Maybe Logan and Bruno were right. Finding a house for Darcy and me should move to the top of my to-do list. Between my mom and Ben —who seemed on the verge of officially moving in together—and now Sandie and Leslie unofficially doing the same, it wasn't such a far-fetched idea anymore.

Chapter 3

Bruno sat at my feet in the meeting room while we waited for Terry, our Community Outreach Director, to take his seat. Usually, I would've dropped Bruno off at the police department, but since this meeting was painfully early, I told Logan his K-9 partner might be a little late that morning.

Honestly, I didn't mind. Having Bruno nearby made the long mornings feel lighter, even if he was more interested in the warm patch of sunlight on the carpet than in my municipal headaches. His tail flicked lazily whenever someone said his name, but otherwise he was perfectly content pretending to nap.

"I get the political issue," said Sophie Parker, our newly appointed Recreation and Programs Director—and easily the best IT mind in the city. "But shouldn't Maple Hollow have to fulfill their commitment to the festival? I'm sure there's a contract that we could use to hold them to it."

"You're right," I said. "There is a contract, but forcing them into it wouldn't end well. We've always gotten along with our neighboring cities, and I don't want to jeopardize that. The last thing we need is a rivalry."

"Or a disaster of a Fall Festival that we get blamed for," Linda added.

Just then, the door burst open and Terry stumbled in, juggling an overstuffed box full of papers.

"Sorry I'm late!" he said, setting the box on the table with a dramatic thud. A few folders slipped loose, scattering papers across the tabletop—and one slid right off, landing near Bruno's paw.

Bruno sniffed it curiously before resting his head on it as if volunteering to guard the evidence.

I smiled. "We'll call that item secured."

Terry straightened, red-faced but grinning. "I couldn't find the updated land maps, so I brought what the archive room had—old city studies, property documents, family registries.

There's a lot of history here, and who knows, maybe something useful."

"Useful like a lost field we could use?" Bert, our Facility Manager, asked dryly.

Terry shrugged. "Or maybe a miracle."

I pulled the paper from under Bruno's chin and opened the nearest folder. Inside were brittle pages stamped with the seal of *Apple Creek Historical Society*. The title read: "Preliminary Study: The Deaport Family Estate and Agricultural Holdings."

A faded black-and-white photograph was clipped to the first page. Three men stood in front of the old farmhouse—two in suits, one in overalls, all wearing the same uneasy expressions. Behind them, the barn looked newer, the kind of sharp-edged structure you only see in century-old photos.

"What's that?" Sophie leaned over.

"Something about the Deaport family," I said, scanning the text below the photo. "It says the family once ran an experimental investment cooperative... focused on agricultural expansion and—" I squinted. "—'missing investment in local gold acquisition'?"

Linda raised an eyebrow. "Gold? In Apple Creek?"

I was about to read further, curious, when Terry reached over and swept a new stack of files onto the table. "Here we go! Land records, topography, all the boring stuff you actually need."

The historical folder vanished under a pile of paperwork before I could ask more.

"Well," Bert said, scanning a document upside down, "I don't see anything in here that could work. But I'm not giving up. I'll check our facilities list—maybe we can rearrange a few sites to fit the festival."

Sophie sighed. "Are you sure the museum's out of the question? It worked for the Art Festival."

I shook my head. "The new director started remodeling the second she took the job. And even if she hadn't, the space isn't big enough for vendors, games, and entertainment."

"When are you planning to talk to the Mayor or the city manager?" Linda asked.

"I'm hoping we can regroup later today and see if we come up with anything," I said. "If not, I'll meet with Martin tomorrow morning. He needs to know before the Mayor does."

Terry groaned. "That's one meeting I'm not looking forward to."

"Me neither," I admitted. Then, forcing the most optimistic tone I could, added, "So far, we've handled plenty of problems other departments wouldn't dare touch. I know we can do this."

They chuckled as they packed up, though none of them looked particularly convinced.

When the door closed, Bruno stood, stretched, and looked up at me with those patient eyes that seemed far wiser than any council vote.

"You're right, partner," I said softly, reaching down to scratch his head. "Something about that farm... Maybe I'll take another look later."

He wagged his tail once, approvingly, and I gathered my notes. "Come on, let's earn our keep—and maybe keep an eye out for a little missing gold while we're at it."

"That is a dangerous animal and it needs to be taken care of!"

Norman Beltran, our Director of Operations and Maintenance, was shouting at a woman who looked to be around my mother's age. She was at least two heads shorter than him, a little on the heavy side, with a cute haircut that blended dark strands with soft grays. But it wasn't her size that mattered—it was the way she stood, arms crossed, eyes narrowed, making Norman look like the one who'd just been scolded by a teacher.

"Wildlife is to be *safeguarded*, Mr. Beltran," she declared, jabbing her finger dangerously close to his nose. "That poor, innocent bird was simply trying to defend itself from you!"

Norman opened his mouth to argue, but his eyes caught mine. "Margaret!" he exclaimed, his voice echoing down the hall. "You run the parks—tell Miss Tony here the city has a policy about keeping wild animals as pets!"

Bruno's ears perked up at Norman's tone. He sat politely at my side, tail twitching in mild curiosity, as if trying to decide whether he needed to break up a fight.

If I'm being honest, when Miss Tony's eyes met mine, I considered turning right around and leaving Norman to his fate. She radiated the kind of authority you couldn't train for—sharp, precise, and absolutely fearless.

"Margaret Willow," she said, her tone softening instantly. A warm smile replaced her glare. "One of the best students of her generation—never got in trouble, unlike some others in this room—and stellar grades."

I blinked, caught completely off guard. "I —uh—thank you?"

She nodded knowingly. "I get that look a lot," she said, sighing dramatically. "I've been working for the school district too many years. Faces stick."

Norman groaned and shoved his hands into his pockets. "Margaret, meet Miss Tony Cooper, the Director of the School District's Registration Office."

Miss Tony cleared her throat, glancing away as if modest about the title. "Who I am doesn't change the fact that you, Norman, need to leave wildlife alone. Am I mistaken, Margaret? Or is it *okay* for residents to harass the animals that live peacefully in this city?"

I opened my mouth to answer, but Norman was faster.

"Peacefully?" he sputtered. "That bird attacked me! I was getting out of my car and it tried to bite me!"

Miss Tony planted her hands on her hips, her voice sharp enough to cut glass. "You shouldn't have parked there! The poor duck was just crossing the lot, trying to reach the pond. And are there not *plenty* of open spaces farther back? It would do you good to walk, Norman. Your belly's getting bigger by the day."

Bruno gave a quiet, polite huff—whether in amusement or agreement, I wasn't sure.

Before Norman could respond, Miss Tony marched to the elevator, pressed the button, and turned on her heel. "Norman Beltran," she said, finger raised, "you should be ashamed of yourself! It isn't enough that we build over their habitats? Now we're harassing them too? Walk more, yell less, and stop terrorizing ducks —especially that poor one!"

The elevator doors slid shut with perfect comedic timing.

Norman groaned and began pacing. "That woman!" he muttered. "You know that *innocent duck* she's defending is *hers*, right?"

I blinked. "I'm not sure what just happened here, Norman."

He jabbed a finger toward the elevator. "For years she's been bringing that mean duck here—pretending it's wild—but everyone knows she's lying!"

I stepped to the window, scanning the courtyard below. Not a single duck in sight. Not even near the pond. "This is the first time I've seen—"

"Of course!" he cut in. "You started in summer. The district only just came back from their luxury vacations." He threw his hands in the air. "And they complain about workload!"

I couldn't help laughing.

He mimicked Miss Tony's voice in a falsetto. "'Wildlife is to be safeguarded, Norman!' You've been warned, Margaret—beware of Miss Tony and her duck."

Bruno tilted his head, giving Norman the kind of patient, unimpressed stare only a K-9 could manage.

Chapter 4

C onveniently, getting to the police department was as simple as walking to the end of City Hall's first floor.

Ben was chatting with the officer at the front desk when Bruno and I stepped inside.

"Well, look who's late to work this morning," Ben said, just as Bruno launched himself forward, tail wagging furiously. Paws up, tongue out—he greeted Ben with his usual enthusiasm.

"Come on, Bruno! Down!" Ben laughed, trying to fend off a full-face lick. "You should know better by now."

I couldn't help smiling. If anyone needed to know better, it was Ben. He was one of Bruno's favorite people, and every reunion was treated like a family celebration.

"Enjoying the peace and quiet around here?" I asked. Then, seeing his frown, I added, "No baby crying in the background?"

Ben puffed and waved a dismissive hand. "Are you kidding? I can't wait to get home and hug that tiny cutie again."

That wasn't quite the response I expected, especially after what Logan had told me the night before.

"Hopefully," Ben went on, "Sandie's tired enough that I can take over for a while."

The officer at the desk chuckled, and I crossed my arms, teasing. "You *hope* she's tired?"

Ben's eyes widened. "Oh no—I didn't mean it like that! Not that she shouldn't feel good—what I meant is—well, come on, Maggie. I missed out on the baby months of my other two grandkids. I plan to overcompensate with Leslie. Unless your mom tells me to stop, I'll be there."

Warmth filled my chest. I must've smiled, because Ben's expression softened even more. He leaned closer, lowering his voice.

"Hope you don't mind," he said. "I've sort of adopted Darcy as my granddaughter. Your mom's hard to pin down when it comes to formalities, and I'm not wasting time on this one."

"I couldn't imagine a better grandpa for Darcy, Toby, or Leslie," I said honestly.

He gave me a quick side hug—probably as much affection as the workplace allowed. "I'll take this officer to his partner," Ben said, reaching for Bruno's leash.

But Bruno didn't budge. He looked between us, tail wagging, clearly torn between his two favorite humans.

"Is Logan busy?" I asked, deciding not to tiptoe around the question this time.

Ben hesitated before handing the leash back. "Something tells me I wouldn't want to be in Detective Forest's shoes right now."

"You'd be right," I said, a little sharper than I meant to.

As I watched Ben smile and ruffle Bruno's fur, something twisted at the back of my mind. What he said didn't line up with what Logan told me last night. For a second, the warmth of the moment dimmed. I wasn't sure if Logan had lied—or if there was something else he wasn't ready to tell me.

I was about to walk deeper into the station when a familiar voice boomed across the lobby.

"Margaret! Boss! Wait!"

Bert was jogging toward me at full speed, a bundle of folders clutched in his hands and an expression that could only mean trouble—or one of his famous "brilliant" ideas.

Bruno perked up immediately, tail wagging again as if he already knew this was about to get interesting.

"So, what do you think, boss?" Bert asked, bouncing on his heels like a kid about to announce a science fair project. "This is the opportunity of a lifetime! We have to take the deal."

I tapped my fingers against the desk, unsure why I was hesitating. Bert wasn't wrong. It *was* the opportunity of a lifetime—probably one of those too-good-to-be-true moments.

"Are you sure he said he won't charge anything? And the concert will be—"

"Yes!" Bert said, cutting me off. "He wants to give back to his hometown."

I nodded slowly, tapping my foot this time. "I just... he's a big deal, Bert."

Bert laughed. "I know you know him as *the* Billy Tolbert, but to me, he's just Bill—

my high school buddy, lazy lab partner, and terrible baseball player."

"Terrible player?" I asked, genuinely surprised. Billy Tolbert looked like someone who'd be good at everything. "And he just picked up the phone when you called him?"

Bert tilted his head, sheepish. "Well, I sent a couple of emails, left a few voicemails and maybe mentioned it was an emergency. But what really got him was Maple Hollow backing out."

I raised an eyebrow. "You told him that? It was supposed to be confidential, Bert."

He threw up his hands. "No, no! I didn't say it directly—he guessed. I called him last week hoping to surprise you with a music celebrity at our festival. Today, I just called to cancel and mentioned we'd lost our location. That's all. Then *he* called back with this idea."

"It's a good idea," I admitted. "We just need to make sure it's actually possible. The farm's a big space, but do we have a capacity limit? Or will we need a special permit?"

Bert sighed, leaning back in his chair. "I checked. As long as we follow the same safety measures we used for the Art Festival at the park, we should be covered."

His expression, however, didn't exactly

scream confidence. I waited for the other shoe to drop.

"The real issue," he continued, "is the historical preservation permit. To use the farm for a crowd that size, we'll need the historian's approval."

"And the council and mayor?"

Bert rolled his hands in the air. "Yes, yes, of course. But they'll be fine. It's the historian you've got to worry about. You don't know him, Margaret—he's a very particular man."

"He's old, but—"

"Oh no, boss," Bert interrupted. "He's *a problem*. His age only makes it worse."

I smiled faintly. "All right. I'll talk to him and—"

"We don't have much time," Bert said quickly. "Bill needs an answer soon—it'll affect his tour schedule."

"All right," I said. "I'll go today."

"You can't go by yourself," he said firmly, then hesitated. "This old man isn't exactly friendly—set on old traditions and all. If you just show up, he will force you to get an appointment that he will delay for weeks—no months!"

I crossed my arms, eyebrow raised. "An appointment? Really?"

Bert winced. "I don't believe that nonsense, but maybe you can bring an official document or better yet, a policeman. Just saying."

I sighed. "A policeman?"

"He's a piece of work."

"Was he your history teacher and you—"

Bert shook his hands and head at the same time. "No! Me? Never... but Bill and our other friend, Terry... he may remember those pranks."

"All right," I said finally. "I'll take Martin with me. We'll talk to him today. We can't risk losing your singer-celebrity-terrible-baseball player-lab partner for this festival."

Bert's grin stretched wide. "Thanks, boss. We're better than those Hollow people any day!"

"Bert! That wasn't the point."

He winked, unrepentant, and headed out the door.

I leaned back in my chair for a moment, exhaling. Bruno, who had been lying quietly near the file cabinet, lifted his head and thumped his tail against the floor.

I smiled and reached for the phone, dialing the city manager's office. "Hi, is Martin available?" I asked. "It's Margaret Willow. Tell him I promise this won't give him a panic attack —probably."

As the line rang, a flicker of unease settled in my chest. Between the farm's sudden relevance in my week and Ben's contradictions of what Logan told me, the day didn't feel right at all.

Bruno gave a soft woof from under the desk, as if to say he agreed.

Chapter 5

Martin did have a minor panic attack, but he was ready in less than twenty minutes. Bruno looked more hesitant than Martin when I left him with Tricia at the police station. Given the number of residents with hair allergies at the senior living, and because he wasn't actively investigating anything, I chose not to bother the residents.

Just an hour after my conversation with Bert, we were walking into the senior living facility on the edge of Apple Creek.

The place was stunning—a sprawling manor surrounded by gardens, tennis courts, mini golf, and even a small amphitheater. Honestly, we could have hosted the fall festival there if not for the limited parking and the cluster of small cabins that some residents rented to stay near their friends. In short, it looked like a college campus for retirees—without the exams.

"Mr. Gray is in the solarium," a friendly woman at the front desk said as she led us down a wide hallway. "He just finished his chess game, so it's a good time to catch him."

The solarium looked like something straight out of a storybook. Sunlight poured through the glass ceiling, illuminating rows of potted plants and hanging ferns that almost brushed the roof beams. Tables and chairs were scattered between the greenery, with a faint scent of citrus and old paper lingering in the air.

The woman pointed toward the far end. "That's him, by the window."

A man with white hair and a wool vest sat there, back slightly bent with age, hands wrapped around a coffee cup. He stared off into the distance, either deep in thought or daydreaming. It was hard to reconcile this peaceful image with Bert's warnings about him.

"Mr. Gray," Martin said as we approached. "I'm not sure if you remember me. I'm Martin Norton, the city manager."

The old man blinked, then smiled as recognition warmed his face. "Martin! Of course. I haven't seen you since early spring. Did you ever find a replacement for Troy?"

Martin straightened, gesturing toward me. "As a matter of fact, yes. Mr. Gray, this is Margaret Willow—probably our best R-Parks Director yet."

I wasn't expecting that introduction, and my cheeks warmed as Walter Gray turned his kind eyes toward me.

"If *this* man says 'probably,' I have no doubt you're excellent, Miss. Willow," he said with a grin.

"Thank you," I replied, smiling. "I'm just doing my best."

"Well," Walter Gray said, gesturing for us to sit, "I've got the rest of the day off, but I imagine you two are busy. What can I do for you?"

Martin pulled out a chair for me before taking his own. Together, we explained the situation—Maple Hollow's withdrawal, the time constraints, and our idea to relocate the Fall Festival to the Deaport Farm. Against my advice, Martin mentioned Maple Hollow's internal issues, which led to a surprisingly long tangent from Walter about how often towns changed their names throughout history.

"As you can see, Walter," Martin said finally, "we're in a bit of a pickle. The farm seems like our best option."

Walter rubbed his beard, considering. His eyes flicked between us before settling on me. "In your expert opinion, Margaret, do you think the festival would work at the farm?" He lifted his cup and took a slow sip. "Because if this is only about pleasing a singer, I'll remind you—celebrities come and go, but historic places remain as our legacy."

I nodded. "You're absolutely right, Mr.—Walter. Our legacy is important. And if we had more time, I'd find a different location. But in this situation, we don't have another choice. The farm is large enough; the barn could hold the concert and dance, and the surrounding land can handle games and vendors. It's near enough that our residents can enjoy it without commuting hassles, too."

Walter leaned back, his eyes thoughtful. "So, the Fall Festival isn't moving there permanently?"

Martin opened his mouth, but I stepped in first. "You're correct, Walter. This would only be a one-time solution. If we host it again next year, we'll look for a more suitable space."

Walter nodded, satisfied. "So, there's still

hope of working with Maple Hollow in the future."

I smiled lightly. "That depends on how their next election goes. Maple Hollow might rename itself out of existence by then."

Martin's jaw dropped, but Walter burst out laughing. "I like this one," he said to Martin. "She's got a sharp wit—and a good head on her shoulders. If you're only asking for a temporary permit this year, you've got it."

Relief washed over me—until Walter spoke again.

"Just make sure those farm animals are out of the barn before the festival," he added. "Neither I, nor the city lawyer, would be comfortable taking that risk."

Martin stood, eager to agree. "Consider it done."

I thanked Walter, and we made our way out of the solarium. The air outside felt cooler, crisper—as if the sunlight couldn't quite follow us out of that glasshouse.

When we reached the car, I shut the door, looked at Martin, and asked, "Please tell me you know where to send those four goats."

Martin glanced over at me, his expression uncertain.

"You don't know?" I pressed.

My face must have given away how serious I was, because his confident smile faltered. He scratched the back of his head and offered a weak laugh. "Upsy."

Neither Martin nor I had a clue where to send those poor goats. Usually, the farm animals we showcased belonged to local farmers we contracted for the season. But these four—our "lucky goats"—were the city's first permanent acquisition, meant to keep visitors coming year-round. I had loved the idea—until today.

"Maybe they really are cursed," I muttered.

To my surprise, Martin didn't laugh. He only nodded gravely. "As long as it isn't voodoo. I won't mess with that one." His expression was as serious as when he delivered budget reports to the mayor on Mondays. "What about Mr. Elliot? I heard he's got property outside the city."

I shook my head. "He sold that when he bought the pub years ago. What about the senior living community? They've got the space, and the residents might actually enjoy the company of the goats for a few days."

"You mean weeks," Martin corrected, folding his arms. "And no. Liability alone would be a nightmare. That place is one broken hip away from a lawsuit. I'm not adding livestock to the mix."

I stopped in the middle of the lobby, scowling. "That's completely inappropriate, Martin. Those seniors are probably in better shape than you and me."

He looked down and cleared his throat. "You're right. Still... their bones aren't as strong as they used to be."

I sighed but didn't disagree. I was still a few decades away from qualifying for the facility myself, and even I could admit that falling these days seemed to hurt more than it used to.

"And goats aren't wildlife," I added. "If Miss Tony heard you say that, she'd be furious."

Martin chuckled. "Did you meet Miss Tony or her duck?"

I frowned. "Norman was arguing with her this morning. What's the story with that duck anyway?"

Martin crossed his arms, leaning against the wall like he was about to tell a big city secrets. "As far as I remember, during the school year we've had a recurring issue—'duck attacks.'"

I blinked. "Duck attacks?"

He nodded. "You haven't seen the reports, have you?"

"I don't think so."

"That's because the attacks only target city staff," he said, lowering his voice. "And they only happen in the City Hall parking lot. Since no residents have complained, the former mayor decided not to publicize it. Didn't want to cause panic—or make the parks department look bad."

I wasn't sure whether to laugh or take notes. "So, this duck just... attacks people?"

"Not *people*," Martin said, grinning. "Mostly Norman, Terry, sometimes Bert. Chief Anderson even looked into it years ago. Turns out it's just one duck—and it belongs to Miss Tony."

I burst out laughing, but Martin didn't join me. He only shrugged.

"I'm serious. It's gotten bad enough that most of us park on the opposite side of the lot. My guess is it has something to do with where they park—or maybe the duck just holds grudges."

"And she still brings it here?"

"My theory," he said, "is that she brings the duck so the neighbors don't complain about her keeping it at home. You know we're not technically supposed to have wild animals as pets."

I smirked. "And I suppose she can't claim it's an emotional support animal since it's technically wild?"

"Exactly," Martin said, looking pleased I'd followed the logic.

"Don't ducks fly away?" I asked.

He shrugged. "She must have a tall fence, a big yard, and a steady food supply. Probably lives better than I do."

Then something clicked. "Wait—what did you just say? A big yard, a fence—Martin, that's it!"

He blinked. "That's what?"

"Miss Tony's house! She's got the space and a fenced yard. The goats could stay there until after the festival!"

I walked towards the elevator, ready to visit the School District floor.

Martin groaned. "Oh boy, I'm not sure she would be in her office anymore."

"Why not?"

"She's gone for the day," he said, checking his watch. "The district follows school hours. She's probably home by now."

I sighed. "Figures. I'll have to wait until tomorrow."

Martin hesitated, then added, "Although I'll probably regret saying this—you could talk to Arthur. He'll know where she is."

I raised a brow. "Arthur, as in *M.E. Arthur*?"

He nodded. "Yes. As in *Medical Examiner* Arthur Cooper—her son."

I felt a little silly. I'd been classmates with Arthur in high school, even shared a science project with him, and somehow had never made the connection. Though now that I thought about it, maybe he'd preferred it that way.

"Keep looking for a backup plan for the goats," I said, heading toward the police department. "This may or may not work—but it's worth a shot."

Martin groaned behind me. "Remind me to retire before the next Fall Festival, will you?"

"You and me, both!"

Chapter 6

I was heading toward the stairs inside the station when a familiar low bark warned me that Bruno was about to launch himself at me.

"Hey, you!" I kneeled to pet him. "I missed you, but you're still on duty, remember?"

"I couldn't tell if *you* knew that," said a familiar voice. Logan was leaning against his office doorframe, half-smiling. "He's wearing his vest, Maggie—but you're rubbing his belly."

I looked down. Bruno seemed unbothered, tail thumping against the tile. "He deserves a break," I said.

Logan stepped closer. "What about me?"

Usually, that question would have sent butterflies through my stomach. This time, I was too irritated.

"Well, I guess the sleep deprivation and chaos in my house have drained my empathy—for two-legged officers, at least."

His smile faded. "Maggie, I'm sorry. I just—"

"Logan," I cut him off, keeping my tone even, "you don't have to make excuses. If you're busy, or if you don't want to see me or my family, just say so."

Guilt flickered across his face, making the silence between us heavier. I stood up, brushed off my knees, and turned to Bruno.

"Stay here, partner. I'll be back at the usual time."

"Are you leaving?" Logan asked quietly. "I thought you were coming to see me?"

There was something in his voice that made me pause—but only for a heartbeat. His hands were deep in his pockets, and he wouldn't meet my eyes.

"I'm not," I said. "I'm here to see Arthur."

Without waiting for an answer, I walked toward the basement. Of course, Bruno followed. I blamed Arthur's candy jar for his divided loyalties.

Footsteps followed us down the stairs. "Aren't you busy?" I asked over my shoulder.

"I am," Logan said, "but in my experience, you visiting the M.E. isn't a good sign."

I stopped to glare at him, but before I could answer, Arthur's voice echoed from down the hall.

"Bruno! Hey—slow down, you're going to—"

The sharp crash of breaking glass cut him off. A heartbeat later, the sound of thousands of tiny things scattering across the floor filled the air.

"Bruno!" Logan shouted, bolting past me. "Back off!"

To my surprise, Bruno obeyed immediately, backing up against the wall, ears low and eyes wide.

Arthur's office was a disaster. Shards of a glass bowl glittered across the floor, mixed with dozens—no, hundreds—of small white pearls that had rolled under chairs and shelves. A faintly sweet, metallic smell hung in the air, like old perfume.

And on Arthur's desk sat a porcelain doll. Its once-pretty face was cracked, one glass eye missing, the other tilted just enough to make my skin prickle.

Arthur kneeled on the floor, trying to

gather the pearls into a pile. Logan stood nearby, snapping on latex gloves.

"Sorry, man," Logan said. "I forgot you were working with the evidence from Tricia's case."

Arthur gave a short, humorless laugh. "You mean the *weirdest* case I've seen in months? Or all my life?"

I frowned. "What happened?"

Arthur sighed, still crouched. "Someone broke into a house last night. But instead of taking anything, they *scattered* these all over the living room—glass jars full of real pearls, seashells, broken marbles and small trinkets. The owner found them this morning with that doll sitting in the middle of her dining table. Both eyes were shattered."

"That's—creepy," I admitted, hugging my arms.

Arthur nodded grimly. "The pearls are genuine. Worth a small fortune, but whoever left them didn't steal a thing. Just... made a scene."

"Arthur," Logan said, exasperated, "that's privileged information. You can't share details like that."

Arthur stood, rubbing the back of his head with one hand and holding a handful of pearls in the other. "Relax. She's here anyway. Might as well save time and hear it from me."

I suddenly wanted to sink into the wall. I wasn't trying to snoop; I just had terrible luck being in the wrong place at the wrong time.

"Is *that* why you're here?" Logan asked, his tone sharper now.

"No," I said, louder than I meant. Both men turned to stare. "I'm here to find Miss Tony. And I just learned she's *your mother,* Arthur. Is that why we always studied at my house?"

Arthur froze, then groaned. "Please don't tell her that. She's... a lot. Always has been. Why do you need to talk to her?"

I tilted my head. "Depends—how big is her yard, and does she still have a fence?"

Arthur squinted. "Is this about the duck? I swear I don't know where she—"

"Not about the duck," I said quickly. "Just real estate."

Logan leaned against the file cabinet, silent but clearly amused.

Arthur sighed. "Her yard's big. The property backs up to the woods on the southwest side of town, and yeah—she's got a tall concrete fence. With a permit, before you ask."

I exhaled. "Perfect. Where can I find her?"

Arthur looked at Logan before answering. "She should be home by now. I could take you."

"What about the weirdest case of your life?" I asked.

Arthur hesitated. "It's fine. I'm waiting for Tricia. Not that I can't work without her, I just need her—for the case. I need her—"

Logan cut in smoothly. "We'll take you there."

I wasn't thrilled, but there wasn't time to argue. "Fine. But we need to go now. I have a festival to plan and a daughter expecting ice cream."

Arthur raised a brow. "What's this all about? Are you buying a house?"

"Maybe," I said with a grin. "But today, I'm making her an offer she can't refuse."

Logan groaned. "The *Godfather*, really, Maggie?"

I shrugged. "Hey, not every day you get to use a classic line at the perfect moment."

Bruno wagged his tail, looking far too proud of himself for causing chaos.

Arthur hadn't been lying—his mother's yard was enormous. If she wanted, she could've fit a mini golf course, a pond, and still had room for a vegetable garden without touching the deck.

"Let me get her," Arthur said, disappearing down the hall and leaving Logan, Bruno, and me waiting in the living room.

For a property that size, the house itself was surprisingly modest. From the front door, you could see straight through to the kitchen, and the staircase rose neatly along the right wall. It reminded me of my mom's place—comfortable and practical, not flashy.

"I hope you have a plan," Logan murmured, stepping closer. "Arthur's mom isn't someone you want to mess with."

I crossed my arms, still stung from his earlier lie about Ben and Leslie. "Are you telling me Detective Forest is scared of this lady?"

He pressed his lips together and nodded solemnly. "Terrified."

Before I could reply, a joyful voice called from the back of the house.

"Oh my goodness!"

We turned as Miss Tony came through the patio door, her energy filling the room. A small, whiteish blur waddled past her feet onto the deck outside.

Bruno stood instantly, muscles tense, ears forward. His leash went taut in Logan's hand.

"Arthur didn't mention he was bringing company," she said cheerfully. "Or that he was coming to see us."

Arthur sighed. "All right, Mom. It's not that unusual. I'm here all the time, and you've met my friends before."

Miss Tony frowned and pointed straight at Logan. "Oh, I know *this* one. Not the best influence."

Behind me, I heard Logan shuffle awkwardly.

"Logan isn't—" Arthur began.

"This young lady, though," Miss Tony interrupted, turning to me. "Now this is the kind of person you should bring home, Arthur. Smart, polite, well-educated, and employed."

My face went warm instantly. I had no idea what to say.

"Margaret, you look just like your mother," Miss Tony said, gesturing toward one of the couches. "Please, sit. Arthur tells me you need to talk to me. Must be important if you couldn't wait until tomorrow... or is it personal?" Her eyes sparkled with curiosity. "I just saw a new file come across my desk with your last name. I assume it's your child?"

I opened my mouth to answer, but she kept going.

"No, don't tell me—I've got this one... Darcy, right?"

I smiled despite my nerves. "Yes, that's my little girl."

"Not so little anymore," she said with a sigh. "They grow up so fast." She gave Arthur a meaningful glance. "Isn't that right, son?"

Her words hit home. She was right—Darcy wasn't so little anymore. She loved school, her friends, and her newfound independence. I loved seeing her happy, even if part of me still pictured the tiny girl clutching her backpack on her first day.

"I'm just glad she enjoys school," I said. "She's made great friends."

"That's wonderful," Miss Tony said warmly. "Her parents must have set a good example. Dedicated students, both of them."

I hesitated at the mention of "parents." In Apple Creek, people rarely mentioned Andrew anymore, and that suited me fine. I wasn't sure how I felt hearing his name implied, especially from her.

"Yes," I said carefully. "Darcy's doing great."

Logan's expression shifted slightly, protective, but Miss Tony seemed oblivious. "So, Margaret," she said, crossing her legs, "what can I do for you?"

I cleared my throat, glancing toward the window and the sprawling yard beyond. That must have triggered something, because Miss Tony's smile vanished, replaced by suspicion.

"I can't do anything about the wildlife in my yard—or the parking lot," she said firmly. "Norman should know that by now. If this is some attempt to implicate me in whatever the city's accusing me of, it won't work."

Bruno's tail stopped wagging. He sat up straighter beside me, eyes flicking between us like he was ready to step in if needed.

"I'm not here about that," I said quickly. "Actually, I want to appeal to your love of wildlife—and ask if you'd be willing to help protect a few innocent victims from the city."

Miss Tony's brows arched. "Protect *who* exactly?"

"This I've got to hear," Arthur said, dropping into a chair and folding his arms. His mother mirrored the gesture but didn't speak.

"For reasons I can't share yet," I began carefully, "the Fall Festival has to move locations this year."

Miss Tony exchanged a knowing look with

both men before turning back to me. "Did something terrible happen in Maple Hollow's orchard? A murder?"

"Mom!" Arthur groaned. "You can't just— what is wrong with you?"

She gestured around the room. "I have three police officers in my living room, Arthur."

Logan started to correct her, but Miss Tony pointed straight at Bruno. "And before you argue, I mean *him*. The handsome one."

Bruno's ears perked up at the compliment, and his tail swished once, as if acknowledging his rank.

I hurried to get back on track. "No murder, I promise. Just politics."

Miss Tony leaned back on the couch, grimacing. "Politics? That's worse."

"Exactly," I said, relieved she'd said it first. "The city needs to relocate the festival to the farm."

"That's actually a good idea," she said thoughtfully. "You can trade apple orchard games for farm ones—similar enough."

"Thank you," I said, taking a breath before adding the hard part. "But there's one problem—the goats. They're city property and can't stay in the barn during the festival setup. We need to find them a temporary home."

Miss Tony's face froze.

"I talked to Norman and Martin," I continued carefully, "and I know how much you care about animals. Who are we to decide where wildlife chooses to live—or rest—or graze?"

"Are you *blackmailing* me?" she asked sharply.

"Not at all," I said, forcing a smile. "That's a crime, and as you mentioned, there are three officers here."

Arthur threw up his hands in mock surrender. "She's right, Mom. Definitely not blackmail."

Logan nodded. "Technically accurate."

Miss Tony's eyes narrowed. For a moment, I swear she was looking straight into my soul. "So what exactly are you proposing?"

"Your duck—"

"She's not my—"

I tilted my head, channeling my mom's best "don't test me" expression. "Please, Miss Tony. Let's be honest. I learned your duck has been guarding the City Hall parking lot for years."

Miss Tony's lips twitched. "Her name is Gertrude."

I smiled. "Gertrude has been keeping our staff safe. For as long as I've been director, I've never seen a single theft report, which makes her an invaluable city asset. As R-Parks Director, I can issue a special permit ensuring Gertrude's continued service—officially."

Miss Tony tapped her foot, considering. "So Gertrude can stay at City Hall. But what about *my* house?"

"Well, you were right when you told Norman we shouldn't interfere with wildlife. Gertrude has every right to live here. The permit simply allows you to transport her safely to and from her 'workplace.' Sort of like how we handle K-9 Bruno."

Bruno's tail thumped proudly at the comparison.

Miss Tony rubbed her face. "And in return, you want me to take care of four goats?"

"Just temporarily," I said quickly. "About three weeks. We'll provide food, and city staff will handle cleaning the yard weekly."

"Goats are big animals, Margaret! I don't know how to care for them."

"They're dwarf goats," I reassured her. "Small, gentle, and absolutely adorable." I reached into my bag and pulled out a brochure from the farm's educational program. "These are Peach, Plum, Nectarine, and Bo."

Miss Tony's eyebrows softened as she studied the photos. "Aww... and Bo!" She lingered for a moment, then straightened with a sigh.

"Two weeks," she said firmly. "No more. And I want that permit in advance."

"Three weeks," I countered, grinning. "And the permit will be on your desk tomorrow morning."

Miss Tony looked from me to Bruno, who had somehow managed to rest his chin on her knee while she'd been negotiating. His brown eyes were pure charm.

"Oh, fine," she said, rubbing his ears. "But only because this officer seems to approve of you."

Bruno wagged once in victory.

Chapter 7

Bert didn't waste a second calling his friend Bill once I told him the news.

Martin, on the other hand, wasn't exactly thrilled when I explained I needed a special permit for Gertrude. But in the end, he couldn't refuse.

If any residents complained, we'd simply argue that years of service to the city—and her invaluable role in protecting our "official" goats —had influenced our decision.

"It's just like how we grant memorial bench dedications," I told Martin. "We don't take just anyone's money and slap a plaque on a bench. We actually evaluate the candidate and decide if the person's been an asset to the city or not."

I knew this well because my mom's request

to dedicate my dad's favorite park bench had been denied. It hadn't made her happy, but she understood. My dad had been a wonderful man, but beyond paying his taxes and enjoying the parks, he'd never worked or volunteered for the department.

Martin sighed. "I suppose it'll work. Just let me know if you need help with anything else. When are you moving the goats?"

"As soon as I arrange transportation—hopefully this weekend. We've got maybe ten days before setup starts. And we still need new activities and games. Any ideas?"

Martin threw his hands up as he backed toward the door. "This one's all yours, Margaret."

I smiled faintly. Typical.

Back at my desk, the to-do list seemed endless—security, rentals, permits, vendors. There was so much to do and nowhere near enough time to do it.

Then Linda's cheerful voice carried in from the front. "Look who wandered all the way up to the third floor!"

I looked up—and froze.

Logan was standing at her desk, hands tucked into his jacket pockets, that infuriatingly disarming half-smile on his face.

Bruno trotted right past him into my office, tail wagging. He brushed against my legs, gave a soft "boof," and then, clearly having a plan, went straight to the sunny patch by the window and flopped down with a sigh.

"I see how it is," I said, watching him stretch out like he owned the place. "Abandon your post for a nap in my office."

He gave me a lazy blink in reply.

Logan knocked lightly on the open door. "May I come in?"

I gestured toward the chair in front of me. "You're already here, might as well."

He sat, resting his elbows on his knees. "I was impressed, Maggie. Not many people could handle Arthur's mom like that."

I tried not to show how much that compliment pleased me. "It was a good deal for both of us."

"An offer she couldn't refuse?" he teased.

I raised an eyebrow. "What can I do for you, Logan?"

He chuckled softly. "At least I'm back to Logan and not 'Detective Forest.'"

I crossed my arms. "Even Linda noticed your absence, so I wasn't imagining it."

"You weren't," he said quietly.

The way he said it made my stomach

tighten. I didn't want to ask—but part of me needed to.

I wasn't going to mention that after Lucy's wedding, after the things he'd said about "doing anything for me," I'd started to believe something might finally change. And then he'd just... disappeared.

When he stayed silent too long, I finally said, "I guess that's good to know?"

Logan rubbed the back of his neck, looking uncomfortable. "It actually—it's complicated. And you shouldn't... I mean, I can't believe I'm back to this kind of problem again. Can I start by saying I'm sorry?"

His eyes met mine, and all my anger melted faster than snow on a spring morning.

"Anything I can do to help?" I asked softly.

He shook his head but managed a small smile. "Do you remember Henry? My best friend?"

"Henry Klauer or Dosal?"

"Mayor Dosal?" Logan said, incredulous. "Seriously, Maggie, you think I hang out with the mayor?"

I grinned. "You *are* older than me, so..."

Logan groaned but smiled. "Henry Klauer. He's been staying at my place for a few weeks now. Actually, he showed up right after Lucy's wedding. Lost his job, didn't know what to do with himself. And since he didn't realize I'm on good terms with your family again, well... he has no idea what kind of mess he's caused."

I tried to think back. Neither Mom nor Sandie had ever mentioned anything bad about Henry. "So Henry doesn't want to see my family? Is he mad at us?"

Logan's gaze sharpened. "You don't know what happened between Henry and your sister?"

My mind raced. "They went to college together. Sandie dropped out, Henry didn't. He became a lawyer, she came home..."

"Close," Logan said. "Except you missed one small part. Henry proposed to Sandie before she dropped out."

I blinked. "He what?"

He nodded. "She dropped out, moved back, and got married a few months later. Henry was devastated. I don't think he's ever really gotten over it."

I sank my head into my hands. "Of course. Not enough that my family already complicated *your* life—they broke your best friend's heart too."

"My life?" he asked, surprised.

"Well, there was all that 'traitor' nonsense

in high school, and—" I shrugged. "You know. Drama."

Logan leaned forward until we were eye to eye across the desk, close enough that I could see the tiny gold flecks in his irises. "Maggie," he said gently, "none of that was your fault. And I should've told you what was going on. I just... panicked. I made fun of Lucy and Sandie for so long, and then I ended up doing the same thing."

My heart softened, the frustration dissolving. "You should've told me," I said quietly. "That's all."

Before he could answer, Bruno let out a low, deliberate *woof*, drawing both our eyes to him. He was sitting up now, head tilted, looking between us with the same patience he used on suspects Logan interrogated too long.

I smiled. "Even Bruno agrees, you should've just talked to me."

Logan laughed, the tension breaking like a spell. "I'll keep that in mind."

He was about to say something else when a loud voice interrupted us.

"Boss!" Terry burst through the doorway, nearly colliding with the frame. I jumped in my seat, and Bruno immediately stood, tail wagging, ready to greet him—or possibly protect me.

"Terry," I said, clutching my chest. "You nearly gave me a heart attack."

Oblivious, he waved a handful of folders. "I've got the vendor list, Sophie's updated budget, and Bert just dropped off security requests and performer demands from this Billy guy."

"Sounds great," I said, uncertain about the rush until Linda shouted.

"Margaret! The Mayor and council are on their way for the emergency meeting now. Let's go!"

I got my folders, fully aware of who was at fault for my memory issue.

The culprit, Logan, stood and smiled, straightening his jacket. "You've got this one, Maggie."

The council meeting had eaten up the entire day and even crept into the evening. By the time I got home, Darcy was already in pajamas, mid-sentence about something that happened at school— and then she was asleep before she could finish it.

I sat at the kitchen counter, surrounded by baby bottles, burp cloths, and a pile of impossibly tiny outfits. Bruno padded in behind me, nails clicking softly on the tile. He gave my leg a gentle nudge before curling up on the rug by the fridge, tail flicking with a sleepy rhythm.

"We had a great day," Mom whispered, her voice low so she wouldn't wake Leslie. "Darcy helped me pick out dresses for her cousin, and we stopped for ice cream on the way home."

"Thanks, Mom." I tried to smile, but Miss Tony's words about how fast kids grow echoed in my head. "This isn't exactly what I pictured when I took the job."

Mom slid a plate toward me, something warm she'd pulled from the microwave.

"I just want to be with Darcy," I said, poking at the food with my fork. I wasn't even sure what was on the plate. "She's growing up so fast. Just like Miss Tony said... and you."

Mom placed her hand over mine, waiting until I looked up. "You're spending more time with her now than you ever did in the city. Of course some days will be busier than others, but she's happy. She's with her grandma. What else could she ask for?"

Bruno gave a soft snuffle in agreement, rolling onto his side.

I chuckled. "You're right."

"This is more you adapting to kindergarten than your job," Mom said.

"If you tell me 'wait for high school,' I'll start crying."

She pressed her lips together, wisely silent.

I took a bite. The rice and vegetables were salty and comforting, and warmth began to push the exhaustion away.

"When you finish that," Mom said, "Darcy got you some ice cream."

That earned a genuine smile. "She's the best."

"Who's the best?" Sandie's tired voice came from the hallway.

She slipped quietly into the kitchen. Unlike Ben, she looked exhausted—dark circles, messy hair, the general dazed expression of a sleep-deprived new mom.

"You okay?" I asked.

"I think she's teething," Sandie said, stealing a forkful from my plate. "Or maybe has colic. Or maybe I ate something weird. Either way, she's waking up every hour."

Mom rubbed her back as Sandie leaned half-asleep on the counter. "You want me to have a word with Paul? Clearly his fault."

Sandie laughed weakly. Mom was the one

to defend him. "Poor Paul. He doesn't look any better than she does."

Sandie stared off toward the living room. "I miss him. He's commuting to Maple Hollow every day. Everyone's rushing to finish projects before winter."

She reached for a small pile of folded baby clothes. "Oh—Ben looks good in this picture," she said, nodding to a newspaper on the counter.

Mom glanced at it. "That's why I saved it. The article's grim."

I leaned closer. The photo showed Ben outside City Hall, microphones clustered around him. Behind him stood Officer Tricia Green.

"What's this about?" Sandie asked, pulling the paper closer.

"Some kind of vandalism," Mom said. "A house on the outskirts of town. The police said someone broke in, but instead of stealing, they left bizarre things behind."

"What kind of things?" Sandie pressed on.

Mom started scooping ice cream as she explained. "Ben said they found dozens of glass jars scattered around the living room—real pearls spilling out everywhere. And in the middle of the table, there was a porcelain doll.

Broken eyes, cracked face. Gives me chills just thinking about it."

Sandie shuddered. "That's awful. Who would do that?"

Mom shook her head. "Ben thinks it's a prank. The family's a little superstitious, apparently. He said the homeowner was hysterical—some woman who kept saying her great-grandmother's spirit was angry."

I felt the air drain from the room. My eyes caught a familiar name in the article, and my heart dropped.

"Thelma and Rose Jacobson," I read aloud.

Mom looked up. "You know them?"

"I just met them," I said, still staring at the print. "They work at the farm."

Sandie's brows knit together as she skimmed the article. "Wait—weren't they the ones who told the legend on the field trip?"

"Yeah," I said slowly. "They're the ones who warned me about Ruth and the goats."

Mom's expression shifted to that look only mothers have—the one that means *don't you dare.*

"Margaret Willow," she began, "if you're even thinking about getting involved in—"

I lifted both hands. "Mom, I swear I'm not. They wanted to talk about the farm, that's all. I have no intention of learning anything about..." I waved vaguely at the paper. "...whatever *this* is. I've got enough to deal with—especially the goats."

Sandie frowned. "Goats? What—"

Right on cue, Leslie's cry echoed from the nursery. Both of them jumped up and hurried off to her rescue.

Silence settled in their absence, broken only by the faint hum of the fridge.

Bruno padded closer, resting his head on my knee. His brown eyes looked up at me with quiet concern, as if he'd felt the tension shift too.

"I know, buddy," I whispered, scratching under his chin. "It's probably just a coincidence."

But even as I said it, the image of pearls spilling across Arthur's office floor—and that doll's crooked, empty stare—wouldn't leave my mind.

Chapter 8

S aturday finally arrived, and I couldn't have been happier to see the weekend.

Moving the goats had turned out to be the easiest part of the entire festival plan. The farm was a great idea, but it came with its challenges—and Billy Tolbert had lived up to every celebrity stereotype. Security requests, special meals, and "creative space" demands had turned the office upside down.

So, sitting on the patio of the bakery with Darcy, surrounded by the smell of coffee and cinnamon, watching the leaves turn gold and red—it felt like heaven.

Bruno was sprawled under the table, chin resting on my shoe, his leash looped around the chair leg. He occasionally glanced up at us with one half-open eye, as if making sure his two favorite girls were staying out of trouble.

"And guess what, Mommy?" Darcy leaned so far over the table she was practically climbing on it. "The teacher told us donut holes come from the *middle* of donuts! I was, like... flabbergasted!"

I laughed, both at her enthusiasm and her vocabulary. "Are you planning to share this amazing discovery with Grandma? Maybe next time, you two can bake donuts."

Her eyes went wide. "Grandma can *make* donuts?"

"Of course she can," came a familiar voice. Sandie stomped across the patio and dropped into the chair across from me.

Darcy squealed and jumped up to greet her, reaching for baby Leslie, who hung comfortably in the carrier against Sandie's chest.

Bruno lifted his head, tail swishing once before resting it again. Even he seemed to know this was a family moment worth staying calm for.

Sandie lowered her voice, though not quite enough. "Did you really think it was a good idea not to *tell me*?"

I blinked. "Tell you what—where donut holes come from?"

She glared. "No, smartypants. That Henry's in town."

"When did you see him? I thought he was avoiding everyone."

Sandie rolled her eyes, freeing Leslie from the carrier. "So you knew! Can you see how I look?"

Darcy, ever observant, tilted her head. "You look fine, Aunt Sandie. Your hair's pretty today."

Sandie's expression softened. "Thanks, sweetie. And your hair looks amazing, too." Then she turned to me. "Well? What do you have to say, Maggie?"

I shrugged. "I really don't know. I haven't seen or talked to Henry."

"But you *have* talked to Logan, haven't you?" she asked, handing me the baby.

I took Leslie into my arms, inhaling that soft powdery scent only babies have. Across the table, Sandie casually stole the rest of my muffin.

"What's the big deal?" I said lightly, bouncing Leslie and smiling at Darcy. "It's not like Henry proposed to you years ago and you never told anyone, right?"

Sandie choked mid-bite, coughing as Darcy's eyes widened.

"Who proposed what, Mommy?"

I handed Sandie my water. "Well, Darcy, when someone wants to ask another person to get married, it's called proposing."

Darcy nodded slowly. "So Uncle Paul proposed?"

"Yes," Sandie said, clearing her throat, "Uncle Paul proposed, and I said yes. That's why we got married."

Darcy frowned. "So you said *no* to this Henry guy?"

I pressed my lips together to keep from laughing.

Sandie pointed at me. "See what you started?"

"You were the one who brought him up," I said sweetly. "Now, why exactly were you late for breakfast?"

Before she could answer, a familiar figure appeared at the entrance to the patio—Henry Klauer, carrying a small bucket of flowers.

Bruno immediately lifted his head, ears up and alert. His tail gave a single flick, the canine equivalent of, *Do we like this guy or not?*

Unlike Logan, who always seemed half-amused by my chaos, Henry had barely acknowledged me back when he dated Sandie. To him, I'd just been the tag-along younger sister.

So when he smiled warmly and walked toward us, I expected him to aim that charm at Sandie.

I was wrong.

"Well, if it isn't a table full of Willow ladies!" he said brightly. His gaze swept over Sandie, but then landed on me. "Maggie, you look wonderful. Logan told me I might find you around town. Mind if we talk?"

He crouched slightly to hand the flowers to Darcy. "And you must be Miss Darcy Willow. These are for you."

Darcy stared at the bouquet, then at me, uncertain.

Henry laughed. "Good instincts. Stranger danger, right? They're from Logan—he said to tell you there's a card inside."

That earned him a tiny nod from Darcy, though she still didn't take them until I gave her a reassuring smile.

"Thank you," I said, standing slightly. "What's this about, Henry?"

"Just a chat," he said smoothly. "I'm sure Sandie can handle the little ones for a few minutes."

He didn't wait for an answer, already heading toward an empty table at the corner of the patio.

Sandie muttered under her breath. "Oh, this should be good."

Bruno watched Henry go, then glanced back at me, tail wagging once like a question mark.

"I know, boy," I whispered. "What could this possibly be all about?"

"Hold on a second," I said, hoping I'd misheard Henry. "You're telling me that your client, Thelma Jacobson, is suing Billy Tolbert for breaking into her house and vandalizing it? With creepy things meant to scare her off the farm?"

Henry took a sip of his coffee and nodded, like he'd just confirmed something as ordinary as the weather. "That's correct. Mr. Tolbert believes he's the rightful owner of the farm and intends to sue the city to reclaim it."

"He what?" I threw my hands in the air. "He's supposed to perform in the Fall Festival concert — for charity, no less!"

Henry nodded solemnly. "I checked the contract. Unless he dies, he's legally obligated to perform. But that doesn't stop him from making his move afterward. I'm sure the concert is just an excuse to inspect the property."

I exhaled, already imagining the mayor's reaction. "How could he possibly own the farm? And what does this have to do with Thelma's house and those... creepy things?"

"That's exactly why I wanted to talk to you." Henry leaned forward, his voice lowering. "Logan said you'd know the farm's background — who owned it, when it changed hands, how the city acquired it. Mrs. Jacobson's records are incomplete, even though her family once held the title."

I folded my arms, thinking. "Her family? So Thelma is a Deaport?"

"That's what she told me. She suspects Tolbert assumed she still owned the place, since she works there. She does work at the farm, right?"

"Yes," I said, sorting through the details in my mind. "She has been around since the educational program and farm opened to visitors."

"Good," he said. "So you're sure the city owns it — that every legal step was taken?"

I hesitated. Having a lawyer ask that question made me second-guess what I'd always assumed. "As far as I know, yes. I can't imagine the city attorney skipping something like that."

Henry sighed, rubbing the bridge of his nose. "That's reassuring. I've got a meeting with Mr. Tolbert and his attorney tonight. I need every bit of background I can get."

"Have you spoken with Mr. Gray?" I asked.

He frowned. "Gray?"

"Walter Gray," I clarified. "Our city historian. If anyone knows the farm's ownership trail, it's him."

Henry nodded and pulled a small notebook from his jacket pocket. He copied the contact info carefully from my phone, each letter neat and deliberate. For a moment, he reminded me of Logan — methodical, serious, but carrying something unspoken beneath the surface.

"I'll check our records at the office and send you what I find," I offered.

He looked up from his notes. "Monday, Maggie. Don't give up your weekend for this."

"Are you sure? Darcy loves going to the office. She'd probably help me color-code files."

He smiled faintly, though his eyes flicked briefly toward the street. A hooded figure was visible in the reflection of his glasses.

"Monday's fine," he said.

I followed his gaze, feeling a small shiver

creep up my spine. The street beyond the patio looked peaceful — a few parked cars, a couple strolling by with coffee cups, the golden leaves swirling lazily in the afternoon wind. Everything looked normal.

Bruno, lying at my feet, suddenly lifted his head. His ears pricked, and he gave a low, almost questioning growl.

I glanced behind me, scanning the row of windows across the street. Nothing. Just reflections of trees and sky.

"You all right?" Henry asked.

"Yeah," I said quickly, though my skin prickled. "Just thought I saw something."

He nodded, finishing his coffee. "Anyway, I'll need to sound convincing tonight — make Tolbert believe I already have every record on the farm. Monday, we'll confirm it for real."

He slid his notebook back into his pocket, then hesitated. "Look, Maggie... I know Logan probably filled you in about me. Tonight's meeting is important — maybe more than I can explain right now. I can't afford to lose this case. Otherwise, I wouldn't have bothered you during family time."

"It's all right, Henry," I said. "If it helps keep the farm safe, it's worth it. Maybe Bert Smith could help — he's the one who contacted Billy about the concert. They went to high school together."

Henry quickly jotted Bert's name. "Perfect. Thanks, Maggie."

I smiled, pushing my chair back. That movement made him pause again, as if something else weighed on his mind.

"I promise I won't keep Logan away from you anymore," he said with a crooked grin. "I'll see you Monday."

He stood, thanked the barista, and left. I watched him disappear around the corner.

Bruno gave a soft whine, tail twitching. He was still staring toward the street, ears perked as if listening for something I couldn't hear.

I reached down to scratch his head. "It's fine, boy," I murmured. "Just a busy afternoon."

As I gathered my things, the distant train whistle echoed through town — low, mournful, and far too long for comfort.

Bruno's ears flicked toward the sound, and my heart did the same.

Chapter 9

Apparently, Logan's flowers had come with an invitation — dessert under the stars with Darcy and me. The note included precise instructions: meet him at City Hall after dark, and don't forget blankets and warm jackets.

Darcy could hardly contain her excitement, chattering the whole drive. And if I was honest, I was curious too.

But the moment I turned into the City Hall parking lot, everything changed.

The night air flashed blue and red from the swirl of police lights. Several patrol cars lined the lot, officers moving briskly between them. My stomach dropped.

I slowed to a stop at the entrance instead of

pulling in. "Mom, can we go?" Darcy asked, her voice suddenly small.

Beside me, Bruno sat up straight in the passenger seat, ears forward, body tense. A low rumble built in his chest — not a growl, but a sound I'd come to recognize as pure focus.

"No, sweetheart," I said, forcing calm into my voice as I opened my door. "Just wait here for a second."

Cool night air rushed in, carrying the faint tang of exhaust and something sharper — adrenaline in the air. I stepped out and locked the doors behind me.

Among the crowd, I spotted Ben, his radio pressed to his ear. His mouth moved fast, but I couldn't catch the words.

Then a patrol car sped past with its siren wailing, making Darcy jump in her seat.

"Maggie!"

Logan's voice cut through the noise as he ran toward me. The sight of the bulletproof vest across his chest — and another heavier one dangling from his hand — made the world tilt slightly.

He stopped just short of me. "I don't want to scare Darcy," he said, keeping his tone even. "Can you open the door for Bruno? I need to put this on him."

My instinct screamed *no*. I shook my head, heart hammering. "Logan, what's going on?"

He took a steadying breath and moved closer, hands gently gripping my shoulders. "I'm not going to lie, Maggie. Something bad's happening, and we need every available unit. Please — open the door so my partner can get ready."

Even in the chaos, he kept his back turned toward the car so Darcy wouldn't see his expression. His eyes, calm and steady, didn't match the urgency in his voice.

"You and Darcy are safe," he said quietly. "Go straight home. I'll call you as soon as I can."

My hands trembled as I reached for the handle. The door clicked open, and Bruno jumped down immediately — alert, controlled, ready.

He didn't bark or pull away. He simply sat beside Logan and waited while the vest was fastened snugly over his shoulders. The transformation was instant — my sweet puppy gone, replaced by a disciplined officer.

Logan bent to check the straps, then leaned to the car window. "Darcy, I'm sorry," he said gently. "We'll have to cancel dessert tonight. But I promise, we'll make it happen soon."

"All right," Darcy whispered, her small hand clutching the edge of her blanket.

"Promise, Darcy," Logan said and then turned back to me.

He took my hands in his, pressing his forehead lightly against mine. "Keep your mom at home," he murmured, "and the doors locked. I'll call as soon as I can."

Before I could answer, he pulled away and jogged toward the cordoned area, Bruno at his side — focused, fearless, the glow of the lights flashing across his vest.

I stood frozen, every instinct screaming to follow, but Darcy's voice pulled me back.

"What's happening, Mommy?"

I forced a smile that didn't reach my eyes and climbed into the car. "I wish I knew, sunflower," I said softly, starting the engine. "I really wish I knew."

As we turned out of the lot, I caught one last glimpse of Logan and Bruno disappearing into the darkness beyond the flashing lights.

My mom's house never had many televisions

— something I didn't appreciate growing up, but tonight, I was grateful for it.

For nearly six hours, Mom had been glued to the one in the basement, watching the live news coverage. I couldn't blame her. Ben was leading the chase. But for me, it was too much.

Every channel showed the same limited scenes: flashing patrol lights blocking the road near the golf course, the long stretch of yellow "CRIME SCENE" tape glowing in the dark, and reporters struggling to fill the silence with speculation.

The last clip looping on repeat showed old footage of Billy Tolbert — smiling at a microphone, shaking hands with fans — a jarring contrast to the headline beneath his name: HOUSE UNDER POLICE LOCKDOWN.

The city alert had come through just as I stepped inside earlier: *Shelter in place until further notice.*

Apparently, the mayor and police chief agreed that a "dangerous and armed suspect" was still at large.

Sandie and Paul arrived a few minutes later. They joined Mom downstairs, while I stayed upstairs, trying to keep things calm for Darcy.

Toby had set up a little blanket fort in the basement, and Leslie slept safe in Sandie's arms. Darcy had fallen asleep on the couch beside me, her head in my lap. The weight of her breathing — slow, steady — was the only sound in the room.

Every creak of the house made me flinch.

When footsteps climbed up from the basement, my heart jumped before my mind could catch up.

The problem with not watching the news was that every sound felt like the start of bad news. Every time Paul came up those stairs, I braced myself for the worst — even though I knew reporters wouldn't have real updates until Ben or the mayor gave an official statement.

"All the same," Paul said softly as he reached the kitchen. "You need anything?"

I shook my head, gently smoothing Darcy's hair. "How's Mom?"

"Quiet," he said after a breath. "Very quiet."

He grabbed a cup, filled it with ice water, then paused by the basement door. "I think she should turn the TV off and rest. Those reporters are just guessing. No one knows anything concrete yet."

I gave him a tired smile and watched him disappear back down the stairs.

When the house settled again, I leaned my head against the couch and looked out the window. The street was mostly dark except for the lone glow of the corner lamppost, its light barely reaching two houses down.

Everything was still. Too still.

At some point, my eyes drifted shut. I didn't know how long I'd slept, only that the soft vibration of my phone under the pillow startled me awake.

The message from Logan glowed on the screen:

Hope I'm not waking you. Can you let Bruno in?

Relief and confusion tangled together in my chest.

I had barely finished reading when headlights swept across the window, flooding the living room.

Carefully, I eased Darcy's head onto a pillow, stood, and tiptoed toward the door, trying not to make a sound.

Somewhere beyond the glass, the faint sound of a car door shutting echoed — followed by a low whine I would've recognized anywhere.

Bruno.

As soon as I opened the door, Bruno trotted up the porch, tail swinging slowly. Relief hit me like a wave. I crouched and wrapped my arms around him, burying my face in his fur for a moment before letting him inside.

He didn't bound for his water bowl or the couch. Instead, he padded quietly over to Darcy, who was still asleep under her blanket, and nuzzled her arm before curling up beside her. She sighed softly, shifting against his warmth.

When I turned back toward the door, Logan was standing at the bottom of the porch steps. The porch light cast deep shadows under his eyes.

"He must be exhausted," he said as I walked down toward him. "It was a long night. He'll probably sleep straight through the day."

I didn't even think — I just moved forward and threw my arms around him. His arms came up around me almost instantly, strong and steady. I rested my head against his shoulder, letting the weight of the night settle for the first time.

He kissed the top of my head, and when I finally stepped back, he looked as drained as I felt.

"Ben asked me to tell your mom he's all right," Logan said quietly.

I nodded, my eyes tracing his face. Bruno might have been the one who'd worked through the night, but Logan didn't look much better. There was exhaustion in his expression, and something darker — worry.

"How are *you*?" I asked, because I knew better than to ask *what happened.*

He exhaled, rubbing his neck. Then he reached for my hand and led me gently toward the driveway, stopping when his back brushed against Paul's car.

"Maggie," he said softly, "please don't get mad at me. I really can't handle that right now. But... I'd rather you hear this from me than on the news."

The night air felt suddenly colder. I wrapped my arms around myself and nodded. "Okay."

He hesitated just long enough to make my

stomach twist. "Bert — your friend — has been arrested."

I blinked. "Bert? What? Why?"

Logan ran a hand through his hair, his expression tightening. "Before I tell you too much, what have you heard so far? I don't know what the news stations are saying."

"Not much," I said. "Just that something happened in Billy Tolbert's house and that there's a dangerous suspect at large. But that can't be Bert."

"No," he said quickly. "That's not Bert. The suspect's still missing. But..." He trailed off and took a step closer, lowering his voice. "You and your family are safe here, Maggie."

I frowned. "Logan, what happened?"

For once, he didn't hide behind his badge. He just looked tired. "There was a shooting outside Billy Tolbert's house near the golf course."

I covered my mouth. My gaze swept over him instinctively, searching for injuries. He caught the look and managed a faint smile.

"I'm fine, Maggie," he said gently.

I cleared my throat. "So... someone tried to break in, and—"

He shook his head, the weariness returning. "I can't give you details. But Ben will release part of it in the press conference soon. We've connected at least three crimes to this suspect." He raised his fingers as he listed them. "One: the possible burglary at the Jacobsons' place — we're still waiting for Mrs. Jacobson to confirm if something was taken from the house this time. Two: a break-in at the senior living center — two guards were knocked out cold. And three..."

He stopped, meeting my eyes. His hesitation was worse than any words. After a long breath, he finished. "The third was a murder in that house. That's where the shooting happened."

A heavy weight settled in my chest. "Henry," I whispered. "Is he all right?"

Logan stiffened, surprise flickering across his face. "Why would you ask about Henry?"

"I—" I sighed, knowing how bad it sounded. "He told me this morning he had a meeting with Billy Tolbert. Said Tolbert wanted to sue the city to reclaim the farm. I told Henry to talk to Walter Gray — the historian — and mentioned Bert had been the one who contacted Billy about the concert. Henry's Thelma Jacobson's lawyer."

Instead of snapping at me for getting involved again, Logan rubbed his hand over his face. "We arrested Henry too," he said quietly. "Maggie... whoever this person is, they murdered Tolbert. Bert and Henry were both in the house when we got there."

"Logan, you know Bert and Henry wouldn't—"

"It doesn't —," he said quickly. "We have to process the evidence. Right now, everything points at them — and the shooter escaping."

My heart sank. "But you don't think they're involved?"

He looked torn, so I reached for his hand, needing him to look at me. "Logan, I'm not angry. Henry's your best friend. I'm asking you, not the policeman."

He gave me a tired smile. "Of course I don't believe it. I didn't believe Paul murdered that council member either, but it doesn't matter."

"It *matters*," I said softly. "You helped Paul then — you'll help them now."

He gave a faint laugh. "That was mostly you."

I felt heat rise to my cheeks, so I looked away and changed the subject. "Can you even stay on this case? I mean, conflict of interest and all that?"

He sighed. "For now, yes. It's too big.

Everyone's working on it. Eventually, I'll probably get kicked off once things settle."

The tired resignation in his tone made something tighten in my chest. I stepped closer and hugged him again. He held on for a long moment, warm and solid despite everything.

When we finally pulled apart, he brushed his thumb lightly over my sleeve. "I've got to head back to the station in a few hours. Try to get some rest, Maggie."

"Of course," I said, though what I really wanted was for him to stay here — safe, with us. "Do you want me to bring Bruno by later?"

He shook his head and smiled faintly. "Good night, Maggie."

I watched him walk down the driveway to his car. The taillights glowed red for a second, then vanished into the darkness.

Chapter 10

By the time I reached the office Monday morning, Apple Creek was buzzing with one thing only—the murder and the suspect still on the loose. My mom had left the news on nonstop since Saturday night, and while I'd agreed with Paul earlier, now I feared we might need an intervention. This kind of thing didn't happen here—but that didn't mean I needed to hear every wild theory in town.

"Let's go, Bruno," I said as I opened the passenger door. He jumped down, stretching before trotting beside me toward City Hall. "We're taking the stairs today. No one ever takes the stairs, so we'll avoid half the gossip."

He wagged his tail as if approving the plan.

At least Bruno wasn't working this morning. The K-9 units had been given forty-eight hours of rest. If anyone asked me, I'd say everyone needed a break. Ben and Logan looked more exhausted than their four-legged partner.

I had just set my purse on the desk when Linda knocked—even though, as usual, the door was already open. Terry and Sophie crowded in behind her.

"Margaret," Linda started, "you *know* Bert didn't do anything wrong."

Terry popped his head around her shoulder. "You must know more than the news is saying. We have to clear this up!"

I folded my arms and looked at Sophie.

"You've got to do something," she said earnestly.

I raised an eyebrow. Before I could answer, Linda added, "You solved the councilman's murder—and the museum case!"

"And the art-heist mess," Terry said proudly. Everyone nodded like a chorus.

I opened my mouth, but Norman's voice carried in from the hallway. "They're right, Margaret. What are you going to do about this?"

Sophie frowned. "Unless you think Bert really did it—but I just can't see that."

Everyone started talking at once. Bruno, who had been lying near my chair, let out a soft *woof*, as if reminding them who was in charge here.

"Everyone, stop!" I said, raising my voice over the noise. Guilt flickered when all those worried eyes turned toward me. "First of all, I didn't *solve* those other crimes—it was mostly luck. But," I lifted a hand before they could interrupt again, "I do want to help Bert. We all do. Let's move to the meeting room so I can actually see everyone."

We shuffled down the hall in a jumble of chatter and half-whispered theories. Bruno trotted beside me, tail brushing my leg, his calm presence helping me breathe.

Martin was already waiting by the back wall when we entered. "Unless you tell me Bert's guilty, I won't believe it," he said firmly.

"Neither will I," I admitted, taking a seat. "But we don't know what evidence the police have. Logan hasn't told me more than what's public."

Disappointment swept through the room like a sigh.

"Still," I added quickly, "Bert's our friend, and we're not leaving him to face this alone. Even if we can't visit him yet, we can help."

Linda leaned forward, a flicker of optimism in her eyes. "So, what's the plan, boss?"

That sounded exactly like something Bert himself would've said, and I couldn't help but smile. "We find out who really owns the Deaport farm."

Predictably, half the room groaned.

"Let me explain," I said and told them about my conversation with Henry—the lawsuit Billy Tolbert had planned against the city, and how the farm's ownership might be the key to everything.

Norman nodded slowly. "Makes sense now. That's probably why those earlier break-ins happened first."

"Maybe," I said. "It sounds obvious, but we can't assume. If we trace the farm's history and deeds, we might uncover something the police will need anyway."

Sophie raised a hand. "What about Bert knowing that singer—Billy Tolbert? Could that matter?"

"Definitely," I said. "But I don't know how we'll find out more if we can't talk to Bert."

"I could hack into his—" Sophie began.

Martin and I spoke in unison: "No illegal activity."

She winced. "Right. But I *can* check old

high-school papers, social media posts, things like that."

"Wait," Martin interrupted, a rare spark in his eyes. "If Bert emailed Tolbert through his city account, we can request access. We'd just need to cite it as festival business."

Everyone turned to stare at him.

"What?" he said, shrugging. "You all signed the data-access waiver last year."

"I'm just surprised that *you* were the one to suggest it," I teased.

Martin smiled faintly. "Let's just say I don't like seeing my people wrongfully accused."

When the meeting broke up, the team left looking more hopeful than when they'd arrived. Bruno stretched under the table, gave a satisfied *huff,* and followed me to the door.

I lingered as Martin adjusted his tie. "If this brings up bad memories—"

He shook his head. "It does. But this time, I don't want to be blindsided. That's what hurt most last time."

I was about to answer when a voice called from the doorway.

"Margaret Willow?"

A tall man in a tan jacket stepped in, extending his hand. "It's so good to meet you in person. I'm Francis Terrance—Maple... Ever...

whatever-we're-calling-it-these-days Hollow's Parks Director."

Bruno tilted his head and let out a short, questioning bark.

"Francis, what brought you all the way to Apple Creek?"

Francis's visit shouldn't have surprised me. After all, Apple Creek had been in the news all weekend, and I doubted the police chase and shooting hadn't made it to national coverage.

"Francis," I said as he stepped into my office, brushing a bit of autumn chill from his coat. "How's the name change going?"

From behind my desk, Bruno stood and padded forward. He didn't growl, but his ears tipped slightly forward as he sniffed Francis's shoes. I'd learned to pay attention to Bruno's reactions—they were often more honest than words.

"I think he's catching the scent of the weird cat that was on the train by me," Francis said with a laugh. He pointed at Bruno. "May I?"

"Sure," I said, watching carefully.

Francis crouched and extended a hand.

Bruno hesitated for half a second, then leaned into the petting, tail wagging. Soon he was pressing against Francis's knee, letting out a pleased huff.

"He's a sweetheart," Francis said, standing to take a seat opposite my desk.

I smiled. "That he is. So... a cat on the train?"

Francis's laugh was deep and contagious. "Oh, yes! The lady beside me had a carrier under her seat. I swear the thing was about to burst—it looked far too small for the cat inside. The moment the ticket guy passed, she unzipped it, and this enormous puff of fur came out, rubbing against my legs like it owned the place."

"How was the rest of the trip? I've heard the train ride from Maple Hollow to Apple Creek is beautiful this time of year."

"I wouldn't know," he said with an exaggerated sigh. "I came up from the city. Family reunion over the weekend. Driving in the city is awful—parking's worse. I took the nighttime train on Friday. Impossible to see anything, and the one this morning up here. That stretch runs along the highway. Nothing scenic there. I'm hoping to enjoy the view on the way back this afternoon."

"Let me know how it goes. I want to take my daughter, Darcy on that route sometime," I said, half to myself. "She'd love it in the fall."

Francis smiled warmly. "You should. Kids remember things like that."

Bruno gave a quiet grunt and sat by my chair, head tilted toward Francis like he was still evaluating him.

"What's his name?" Francis asked.

"Bruno," I said, stroking his ears.

"Ah, Bruno. Handsome name. He must be tired after the weekend—I saw on the news that Apple Creek called in every available officer, even the K-9 units."

I frowned, glancing at Bruno. He wasn't wearing his vest today, so there was no visible clue. "How did you know he's K-9?"

Francis leaned back, hands steepled. "Well, you don't see many bloodhounds lounging in government buildings without causing trouble. I figured he wasn't just a pet—too well-behaved for that. After what happened this weekend, I assumed he's just taking a well-deserved day off."

I nodded, though something about his easy answer tugged at me. It was perfectly logical... maybe too logical.

Francis didn't linger there long. "Please tell

me you don't have to cancel the festival! I've been worried sick about it. The vendors were so excited—it's one of their best events of the year."

He sounded genuinely regretful, just as he had on the phone a few days earlier.

"Unless the mayor changes his mind, we're still hosting it," I said. "The concert's off, of course. But the festival itself is still on schedule."

Francis nodded gravely. "Such a tragedy. Still, I'm glad it's moving forward. Where's it going to be? I'd love to see the new site—maybe steal the idea for our next event back in Maple—Ever Hollow." He winked.

I laughed. "Well, as long as you've got a historical farm handy."

"The farm!" he exclaimed. "Brilliant. I haven't been there in ages. It fits perfectly with the fall theme. Any chance I could get a tour? I'd love to ask a few questions—strictly professional, of course. Though my inner history nerd would enjoy it too."

I was about to delegate the task to Terry, but then I hesitated. If there was anything at that farm that could help Bert and Henry, I wanted to find it myself.

"I actually have to head over there now," I said. "You're welcome to tag along."

Francis beamed. "I'd love that. But please, if you're busy—"

"It's no trouble," I said, grabbing my coat. "Bruno and I could use the walk."

Bruno stretched, tail swishing, ready as ever.

As Francis held the door open for us, the scent of autumn drifted in—crisp air, fallen leaves, and something faintly metallic, just like in Arthur's office.

"Stop!"

The shout came from across the farm just as I was trying to open the barn's door. I didn't think it was directed at us until it came again, louder and closer.

"That's locked—closed to the public! Can't you tell it's locked?"

Francis and I turned around just in time to see Thelma Jacobson rushing toward us, her coat flapping behind her. She stopped short, catching her breath.

"Oh no," she said, lowering her voice and

pressing a hand to her chest. "I'm so sorry. I didn't recognize you. I—well, I'm just trying to keep people out of here."

I let go of the latch and took a step toward her. "Why is it closed? When I came with the school group, they were able to see the inside."

Thelma lifted her hands, shaking her head as if searching for the right words. "I believe the goats— they don't want them moving—"

"We moved the goats this weekend," I said, unable to hide my annoyance. "Isn't that what you wanted?"

Her eyes dropped to the ground, and she took a half step back, her shoulders tensing.

Before she could answer, Francis interjected. "I thought the barn was empty." He glanced toward the wooden doors, rubbing the back of his neck. "Moving animals must've been a project. Do you partner with local farmers for that?"

I explained how we handled the move ourselves and arranged temporary housing and care during the festival, since the city owned the goats. Francis nodded thoughtfully, making a few notes on his phone.

"Ever Hollow's been trying to strengthen our recreational programs," he said. "Lots of requests for goat yoga lately. How do you like working with goats, Ms. Jacobson?" he asked, smiling. "Oh—Francis Terrance, Parks Director of Maple—Ever—whatever we're calling it Hollow."

I realized I'd forgotten introductions. "I'm sorry. Francis, this is Thelma Jacobson, she works part time here."

When she finally looked up, her face was pale. Her hand trembled slightly as she shook his. "Nice to meet you," she murmured. "The goats are fine, I suppose. I don't see them often —I'm usually in the farmhouse."

Her voice was soft, nothing like the confident tone she'd had seconds earlier. Bruno noticed too. He stood beside me, ears forward, watching her with quiet intensity.

Wanting to put her at ease, I asked gently, "How are you feeling, Thelma? After the break-in, I mean. I heard what happened and hoped nothing valuable was taken."

Thelma froze, her fingers twisting together. "I... I'm fine," she said too quickly. "The police said it was probably just kids. Nothing's missing, really. It's all still there."

She gave a fragile smile, but her eyes darted toward the barn—nervous, watchful.

Francis noticed too but didn't press. "Do

you think we could see the barn?" he asked instead. "I'm curious about the layout."

"No!" Thelma's shout startled all three of us—Bruno jumped, barking once before settling at my leg.

"Sorry," she said, flustered. "I didn't mean to yell. It's just—Mr. Smith closed the area... he's our facilities manager."

Francis tilted his head. "You said Mr. Smith locked it? Did he help moving the goats? Why would he kept it close?"

Thelma's hands fidgeted again. "Yes—well, no Mr. Smith put the lock because of the festival stuff. Now is locked under police orders, because of Mr. Smith's arrest."

I stepped in before she unraveled further. "It's all right. We don't need to go inside. Without the concert, the barn isn't part of the festival anyway."

Francis nodded agreeably. "Fair enough. If it's not part of the event, no harm done. And the goats aren't here—that's a shame. The child in me always enjoys meeting farm animals."

We started back toward the parking lot. The wind carried the faint scent of hay and sawdust, and the quiet creak of the barn's weathered boards followed us.

As Francis was walking towards the car, I

saw something shimmering—a little sparkle close to the dirt path.

I crouched down and brushed aside a few dry leaves. A smooth, round bead. It looked like a pearl, maybe from a craft project—or maybe not. The memory of Arthur's office flashed in my mind: the jars, the doll, the pearls.

Bruno gave a short bark, waiting by the car door, tail wagging but posture tense.

"Everything all right?" Francis asked.

"Nothing to worry about," I said softly, slipping the pearl into my pocket. "Just a piece of someone's craft project. Do you want a ride to city hall or the train station?"

"The train station will be perfect, Margaret." He looked around the farm with a smile on his face. "I'm sure our vendors will be thrilled about this venue. You've done a wonderful job."

"Thank you," I said, though my thoughts were still back at the barn.

As we pulled away, I caught one last glimpse of Thelma standing near the entrance, her arms crossed tightly over her chest, her eyes fixed on the locked doors—as if afraid of what might be waiting behind them.

Chapter 11

For the first time in my life, I spotted Gertrude in the parking lot.

As Bruno and I were heading back into City Hall, I noticed a duck with soft brown-spotted feathers waddling along the far path by the building. Of course I had to look closer. Tightening Bruno's leash, I followed at a polite distance.

Norman's warning came to mind, but Gertrude didn't seem bothered by us. She moved with the slow, confident pace of a bird who owned the place. I called out softly, "Hey, Gertrude," just to test it, but she didn't react — which could've meant she ignored me... or I wasn't saying it quite right.

Bruno tilted his head, ears pricked, but stayed calm. We followed her to the small pond, where she slipped into the water with graceful ease.

"Cute," I murmured.

Bruno, however, wasn't looking at the duck. He was fixated on a car parked near the edge of the lot — the same spot Miss Tony had scolded Norman about for blocking Gertrude's route.

I sighed, half expecting the car to be covered in duck revenge, and wasn't disappointed. White splatters dotted the roof and windshield. "Well," I said to Bruno, "looks like Gertrude and her friends made their point."

Still, something about the car made me pause. The bottom edges and tires were caked with a thin layer of pale dust — thicker and muddier than normal road grime. Bruno sniffed along the bumper, tail wagging slowly, then circled to the back.

The dust reminded me of soil by the farm.

"Margaret!"

I straightened at the sharp tone. Ben was standing near the building entrance, arms crossed, expression stern. Even Bruno froze mid-step, leaning subtly toward me for reassurance.

"Ben," I said carefully. Maybe I'd accidentally taken Bruno when he was supposed to be working, though I was sure Logan had told me he was off duty. "Everything all right?"

"Inside," Ben said, jerking his head toward the doors. "A word, please."

That didn't sound good.

As soon as we stepped inside the police station, the noise seemed to quiet. Conversations dimmed. Heads turned. It was strange — I'd been in and out of this place countless times to pick up or drop off Bruno, but this felt different.

Ben didn't stop at his office. He walked straight past it, down the hallway, and opened the door to one of the small interrogation rooms.

For a moment, I froze. The last time I'd been in here, it was to help Paul clear his name — and the memory wasn't exactly comforting.

Still, Ben didn't ask me to leave Bruno outside, so how bad could it be? Bruno followed close, sitting right by my chair the second I sat down.

Ben closed the door behind us. "Why, Margaret?"

My brow furrowed. "Why *what*, Ben? You're going to have to be more specific."

He exhaled, rubbing a hand through his hair. "You know Henry Klauer — that much I expected. What I *don't* understand is why a high-profile lawyer like him just named you as his representative and refuses to speak with anyone else."

I blinked. "He *what*?"

Ben leaned forward, bracing his hands on the table. "Henry named you his attorney. He says he'll only speak to you. So, you tell me — why?"

My mind went blank. "Ben, I swear I have no idea. Henry and I only spoke once — on Saturday — and I already told Logan that. Before that day, I hadn't talked to him since college. Probably longer."

He studied me for a long moment, searching my face. Bruno shifted closer to my feet, pressing gently against my leg like he could sense my heartbeat speeding up.

"Listen, Maggie," Ben said finally, his tone softening just a fraction. "This is a major investigation. The last thing I need is to explain to the mayor, the council, or the press why a civilian's involved." He sighed and rubbed the bridge of his nose. "So if there's anything — anything at all — you haven't told us, now's the time."

I shook my head, hands open. "I'm telling

you the truth, Ben. I don't know why Henry would do that."

Ben stared for another moment, then straightened and walked to the door. "Stay here for a minute," he said, and stepped out.

The door clicked shut behind him.

For a long moment, the only sound was the hum of the ceiling light. Bruno lifted his head, ears turning toward the hallway.

"Yeah, boy," I whispered, scratching behind his neck. "I don't like this either."

The minutes felt endless before the door finally opened.

Ben stepped inside, guiding Henry in front of him. Henry still wore the same suit from Saturday — wrinkled, rumpled, and looking as tired as the dark circles under his eyes. But what stopped me cold was the metallic click of the handcuffs as Ben fastened them to the table.

He checked them twice, then gave me a look — the kind of warning only Ben could manage without saying a word — before leaving the room.

Henry stared down at the cuffs, rubbing his wrists against the chain. "He just put them on," he said quietly. "I'm sure he's worried about you."

I didn't answer. I just nodded slightly, appreciating Ben's concern even as my stomach twisted. I didn't believe Henry had done anything wrong — but seeing him like that made everything feel heavier.

"What's going on, Henry? You're the lawyer, not me."

He stayed silent for a moment, gaze fixed on his hands. When he spoke, his tone was low and strained. "I know I'm in deep trouble, Maggie." He looked up at me then, eyes hollow. "I didn't do it. But... I get why Logan had to arrest me. You helped him once, didn't you?"

I frowned, caught off guard.

"Logan," Henry said, half smiling. "Years ago, when he got arrested. It was you who cleared him."

It shouldn't have surprised me that Logan had told him — they'd been friends for years — but the mention still sent a flicker of confusion through me.

"It's all right," Henry said, reading my face. "You did a great job. Real police or not." His smile faded. "And I was hoping you might do the same for me."

I leaned closer to the table. "Henry, I'm sure Logan will help you. We all will."

He shook his head. "Logan has to do his job. And as a lawyer, I know how bad this looks. Without someone trying to clear my name, I'll end up in prison for conspiracy and murder. That's a long sentence, Maggie."

The fear in his eyes reminded me of Logan's that night by the patrol cars — weary, haunted.

"Henry, I really don't know much," I said. "I can't promise anything."

He reached across the table and gripped my hands. The cuffs clinked softly as he leaned forward. "I just need to know someone's actually trying to help me — not just solve a case."

"I'm sure you're not just a case to Logan."

Henry nodded. "I know. But this one's on me."

I took a slow breath. "Tell me what happened."

He rubbed his temple, trying to gather his thoughts. "After we talked Saturday, I decided to visit Mr. Gray before meeting Tolbert that night. I didn't have an appointment, so I just drove there — straight from the bakery."

That lined up with what I knew, but my heart was already pounding.

"On the way," Henry continued, "Thelma called. She was panicked. Said her niece was missing and didn't know if she should call the police since it hadn't been forty-eight hours. I went over to help. Turns out Rose wasn't missing at all — she was at the farm volunteering. Thelma forgot she'd signed up for the weekend shift."

I frowned. That didn't make sense. The farm's weekend volunteers were supposed to be adults only, not high-schoolers. I made a mental note to check that later.

"By the time I left Thelma's, I was starving," Henry went on. "Stopped at a gas station on the way to the senior center. Grabbed some junk food — the kind Sandie would've lectured me about."

The way he said her name made my chest ache. I didn't know exactly what had happened between them, but I knew the wound was still there.

"I remember getting back in my car," he said, voice faltering. "Turning the engine on... and then nothing."

I leaned forward. "That's the bandage on your forehead?"

"I think so. I have flashes — weird smells, like gasoline or fumes — but nothing clear. Whoever hit me must've shoved me in the trunk."

He looked up, seeing doubt in my expression. "Yeah. That look. Everyone gives me that look. I swear, Maggie, I didn't break into Mr. Gray's home or kill Tolbert. And I definitely didn't shoot at the police!"

I lifted my hands. "Okay, okay. So you don't remember anything until when?"

He tried to gesture, but the cuffs stopped him with a metallic clink. "I remember waking up in my car. The dashboard lights were on, blue and red flashes all around. My head was spinning. I barely realized what was happening until I opened the door and practically fell into the street."

He swallowed hard. "That's when I heard shouting — guns cocking — sirens everywhere. Then I saw the barrel of a shotgun pointed right at me. I didn't know it was Logan until he grabbed me and said my name."

He exhaled, shaking his head. "He arrested me after that. I think there were some swear words mixed in with my Miranda rights, but I can't blame him."

I rested my elbows on the table, cradling

my head in my hands. "Henry, someone obviously assaulted and kidnapped you."

He gave a bitter chuckle. "If I were a prosecutor, I'd call that too convenient — especially since there's no proof. And the worst part? There's gunpowder on my hands, and my car had a gun I've never seen before."

Beside me, Bruno let out a low rumble, his head resting against my leg. I reached down, brushing his fur to calm us both. Henry was in serious trouble.

"What about Bert?" I asked quietly.

Henry shrugged. "Met him for the first time in holding. His story's just as bad — says he was talking to Bill by the main door when he got knocked out. He woke up inside the house, panicked, and threw a vase at the first officer he saw. I can't blame him. Waking up to an entire police team yelling orders? I'd have done the same thing."

He closed his eyes, voice dropping to a whisper. "What do you think, Maggie? Will you help me?"

I reached across the table and touched his cuffed hand. "I'll do my best, Henry. I can't promise anything, but... I'll try."

He smiled faintly, the tension in his shoulders loosening. "That's all I needed to hear. No wonder Logan cares so much about you."

That made my stomach flutter, and I stood quickly before he could see it.

At the door, I turned back. "What do I tell Ben? I'm not a lawyer. I don't have client privileges or whatever it is."

Henry chuckled softly. "You can tell him everything. I haven't told you more than I told them already. I hope you believe more than they did."

Chapter 12

Ben was standing near the front desk, arms crossed, his expression serious enough to remind me of how he used to look years ago — back when the person in trouble had been Logan.

"I shouldn't have to tell you how dangerous this case is, right, Maggie?"

Bruno trotted up to him and sat obediently at his feet, looking up expectantly. The action softened Ben's stern face into a faint smile. Still, the way he'd pulled me aside — and his tone — made my stomach tighten.

"I know, Ben," I said, folding my arms. "There's a dangerous suspect at large. It's all over the news. Which, by the way, is all my poor mother watches these days. I don't have to tell *you* how dangerous it is to upset my mom, do I?"

Ben sighed and crouched down to scratch behind Bruno's ears. "Believe me, I know. Which is why I'm even more worried now. How am I supposed to keep this from your mom?"

I chuckled, partly to ease the tension. "Relax. Henry didn't tell me anything new. He just asked me to—" I caught myself before finishing. Telling Ben that Henry had asked me to look into the case wasn't a smart idea. I pivoted smoothly. "—to check on Logan. Make sure he's all right. And that Sandie doesn't find out about all this."

"Sandie?" Ben stood again, frowning. "What does she have to do with the case?"

"Nothing," I said quickly. "But they were high school sweethearts. I think Henry still cares about her."

Before Ben could respond, Tricia walked in. She looked as tired and tense as everyone else in the station. "High school sweethearts? Who?"

The bead in my pocket came to mind, and I jumped at the chance to change the subject. "My sister and Henry. Anyway—check this out." I pulled out the small pearl-like bead I'd found at the farm and handed it to her.

Tricia turned it over in her fingers. "What's this?"

"I found it near the barn," I explained. "It reminded me of those creepy jars Arthur was working with last week. Hard to forget something like that. When I saw this on the ground, I got the same feeling."

Tricia raised an eyebrow, clearly skeptical. "Creepy, sure, but you don't have to worry. This one's not real. The ones from the jars were old, genuine pearls — and very expensive."

That made me exhale in relief. "Good. I figured it was probably from one of the craft programs at the farm. But after everything, I'd rather make sure."

Ben straightened, rubbing his temple. "Just... stay out of this one, Maggie. Promise me."

"I'll try," I said, which wasn't exactly a promise but seemed to satisfy him.

Sensing the conversation was ending — or maybe picking up on the tension — Bruno gave a short bark and nudged my leg.

"Right," I said, smiling faintly. "Come on, partner. Let's see if the department's figured anything out about the farm ownership."

Ben and Tricia exchanged a look as I turned toward the elevator. I pretended not to notice.

If they thought I was going to sit quietly while my friends were accused of murder, they clearly didn't know me well enough.

"Absolutely sure," Terry said, standing tall with his hands on his hips. "The city lawyer had everyone review every piece of paperwork from the sale about a year ago. It's clean. The farm belongs to the city—no questions about it."

I tapped the table, thinking. Apparently, Thelma had been telling the truth. Her family, the Deaport's, had owned the farm since it was built more than a century ago. She'd been the last of the family, struggling to maintain the property. Not wanting to see it demolished—and since it wasn't yet historically protected—she'd sold it to the city.

From everything I could tell, it had been a good deal for both sides. Maybe she'd even lost money by not selling it privately. Still, I could imagine how expensive that place must have been to keep up.

"And nothing connected to Tolbert?" I asked.

Terry shook his head. "Not a trace. I think it's just one of those celebrity delusions. But whoever emptied a gun into him at close range... that sounds personal."

I had to agree. The news reports confirmed that Billy Tolbert had been shot multiple times at near point-blank range.

"I think I found something on Bert's emails," Sophie said, stepping into my office.

Terry and I turned instantly toward her.

"You see," Sophie began, setting a stack of papers on my desk, "most of the messages were from Bert. He was doing his best to get Tolbert to perform at the festival. There are some references to high school memories—things Bert was trying to use to convince him."

She took a step back. "It felt weird reading some of it."

"Was Bert being inappropriate?" Terry asked.

Sophie shook her head. "Not at all. He was polite, professional—just trying hard. The odd part is that Tolbert ignored him for weeks. Then, when Bert mentioned the festival might be canceled, Tolbert suddenly replied—and offered the *farm* as the concert location."

I frowned. "That's right. Bert said it was Tolbert's idea."

"Yes!" Sophie pointed to the top email. "Here—he wrote that the barn would be perfect for the concert, even talked about using the farmhouse for an after-party. He offered to handle setup for both the barn and the house."

Terry crossed his arms. "Maybe he wanted to inspect the property before trying to claim it. Pretend he had some personal connection to it."

That lined up with what Henry had said. But Sophie kept going, and what she read next made my stomach tighten.

"He wrote about playing on the farm as a kid," she said quietly. "He said he and some friends used to camp out in the barn's hayloft." She grimaced. "Then he told Bert how much fun it would be to recreate those nights—just older now, with a little music and nostalgia."

I didn't like that Tolbert knew so much about the farm. Sure, everyone in Apple Creek grew up hearing about the legend, but this felt different—too specific.

"Bert didn't mention that offer to me," I said.

Sophie nodded. "In his reply, Bert blamed the mayor and council for micromanaging everything. We know that's not true. I think he found Tolbert's sudden enthusiasm suspicious."

Terry rubbed his chin. "He probably did. Bert was no fool. He must've sensed something was off."

Sophie hesitated before adding, "He agreed to meet Tolbert Saturday evening. In one email he wrote—'I'll make you understand my point once and for all.'"

The phrasing made my heart sink. "And we don't know what that point was."

She shook her head. "No. Maybe they talked by phone, but there's nothing written."

I sighed, leaning back in my chair. This wasn't going to help Bert. If anything, it made him look worse. The idea of him meeting Tolbert right before the murder was exactly what a prosecutor would latch onto.

After a few exchanged theories—most of them far-fetched—Terry and Sophie left my office.

The sun had started to dip, the golden light painting long shadows across the floor. I stood to gather my things when something rolled out of my pocket and hit the tile—a soft *clink* followed by a faint bounce.

The pearl.

It rolled towards the wall, and then jumped up before I took it.

I stared after it, uneasy. Maybe it wasn't a real pearl, and maybe the jars weren't connected to the murder—but somehow, everything kept circling back to that farm.

Bert had locked the barn. Tolbert had written about it. Thelma had insisted no one go near it—and had practically panicked when we tried.

Too many threads tied to one place.

I looked down at Bruno, who had lifted his head from his nap and was watching me with alert, expectant eyes.

"What do you think, Bruno? Should we go check the farm?"

His ears perked up immediately, tail flicking once. Then he looked toward the window, as if he understood what I was suggesting—and wasn't entirely sure it was a good idea.

"Yeah, I get it," I said softly, clipping on his leash. "We shouldn't go alone after dark." I gave him a gentle scratch behind the ears. "Let's see if Logan's free to come with us."

Bruno gave a low, approving *woof,* and for a moment, it felt like we were both holding our breath—waiting for what came next.

Chapter 13

I climbed out of Logan's car with the farm keys in hand, trying not to think about legends as the full moon cast silver light across the fields.

"So let me get this straight," Logan said, shutting his door. "A dark ice rink? No problem. An empty museum? You're fine. But a barn—with goats—is where you draw the line?"

Since the place was empty, he didn't bother leashing Bruno. The bloodhound bounded ahead, nose to the ground, tail wagging at the scents only he could read.

"This is different," I said firmly. "And the goats are gone, remember?"

I took a step forward, then paused to wait for him. Logan laughed at me.

"What? This place has a terrible legend. Goats that lead you to Ruth so you never come back? No thank you."

Still chuckling, he offered me his arm. I took it without hesitation—this time not because of butterflies. Apparently, even they drew a line at haunted barns.

"Margaret Willow," Logan teased. "I never pegged you as superstitious."

"I'm not!" My voice came out a little too sharp. "It's just... well, why mess with things, you know? Just in case."

Bruno trotted back toward us, ears up, tail wagging, completely unconcerned with the chill in the air or the shadows stretching across the farm buildings. Unlike me, he seemed perfectly at home.

At the barn door, Logan reached for the keys I was clutching. "Still laughing at me," I muttered.

"Now I see why you never came with us in high school," he said, turning the key over in his hand.

I opened my mouth to defend myself, then closed it again. He wasn't wrong. Back then, I'd been more afraid of trouble than legends. And now? Between Thelma's panic, Rose's terror, and those jars in Arthur's office... my nerves felt justified.

"Remind me," Logan said, "who locked the barn?"

"Thelma told Francis and me that the *police* had closed it."

"The police?"

I nodded. "That's what she ended with. Francis caught her changing the story. According to her, Bert locked up first for the festival, and then the police kept it closed after they arrested him."

"Why Bert?"

"He's Facilities Director. It's his job to manage city buildings used by R-Parks programs. That's why I have this key."

Logan held it up. "Except this won't work. Because this padlock isn't city-issued."

I frowned. "How do you know?"

He tugged at the padlock. It didn't budge. "Your key doesn't fit it."

Of course I had to try myself, rattling the lock uselessly. "Could Bert have swapped the padlock?"

"Maybe," Logan said, "but why?"

It didn't make any sense. "After we moved the goats, the barn was supposed to be prepped for the concert." I lowered my voice. "Thelma was furious when Francis and I headed this way. When she realized who we were, she practically panicked."

Logan studied the doors for a moment, then moved along the side of the barn. Bruno followed eagerly, nose pressed to the ground. I hurried to keep up.

"What are you doing?" I asked.

"Looking for another way in," he said, his tone serious now.

We stopped near the corner. Logan pointed upward. A small, cracked window sat high above, coated in dust. The pale powder gleamed in the moonlight—eerily white, just like the residue I'd seen on the car in the parking lot.

"Maggie?" Logan asked quietly.

"I saw a car in the City Hall lot today," I said quickly. "Parked near Gertrude's side. It was covered in that same whitish dust."

He smirked. "You assigned part of the parking lot to a duck?"

"Logan," I snapped. "Did you see it or not?"

He rubbed his jaw, thinking. "Yeah. Dirty, dusty. Just like this."

"Exactly." I pointed at the window.

Instead of dismissing me, he frowned and strode back toward the front of the barn. I had to jog to keep up.

"Stay back," he said, picking up a large rock.

"What are you doing? Isn't this trespassing?"

He swung the rock hard against the lock. Once. Twice. The hook snapped free.

"Isn't this city property?" he asked, prying the padlock off. "And aren't you the one who runs it?"

Before I could answer, he pulled the door open and stepped inside.

Bruno darted past me, vanishing into the shadows.

And suddenly, I was alone in the moonlit yard. The farm was too quiet, the woods too close, every shadow too deep. The prickling sensation of being watched crawled up my back.

I wasn't sure if I stepped into the barn to see what was happening—or just because I couldn't bear to stay outside by myself.

Logan's flashlight beam cut through the darkness, casting long, ghostly shadows across the barn. I wasn't sure what I expected—certainly not this: a wide, empty stretch of stalls, a loft thick with hay that blanketed half the ceiling, and a shaky wooden ladder leading up to it.

"Any chance there's a working light in here?" Logan asked, scanning the rafters. "I'd like to check up top, and I doubt you want to stand around down here in the dark."

He wasn't wrong.

I wandered toward an old workbench tucked against the far wall. A small desk lamp sat at the corner; when I switched it on, a soft amber glow spread across the surface, pushing back the shadows just enough to feel almost safe. The neatly lined-up tools and the random teacups with nails really caught my eye.

Up close, I noticed the bench was strangely spotless, the wood smooth from years of use. The drawers were carved with some kind of pattern—tiny shapes I couldn't quite make out in the dim light, maybe animals, maybe just decoration—and each had an old metal handle with a rusted flourish shaped like a fancy *D*. It was probably nothing, but something about the quiet care in those details made the whole thing feel... personal.

Above me, the old boards creaked as Logan climbed the ladder. "You might want to come up," he shouted.

Before I could answer, Bruno's low growl rumbled through the barn. It came from the stable where the goats had once been kept—a deep, warning sound I'd rarely heard from him.

"Stay there, Maggie," Logan ordered, and the ladder groaned as he started down.

Bruno barked sharply, once, twice, then lunged at the stable wall. The heavy thud of his body hit the boards, followed by a crack.

"Bruno!" I shouted, but the sound of splintering wood drowned me out. Within seconds, the boards gave way, collapsing inward. The barn trembled; dust exploded into the air, swallowing everything in a gray cloud.

"Bruno!" I coughed, rushing forward—but before I could reach him, he bounded toward me, tail wagging, eyes bright. I dropped to my knees and checked him over, relief flooding me.

"I'm fine too," Logan said dryly, brushing sawdust from his jacket as he passed.

"I *knew* you were fine," I said, then muttered, "If you weren't, I'd be buried under those boards by now."

Logan kneeled by the broken wall, flashlight beam slicing through the dust. The stable wall still stood, but shattered boards lay across the floor.

"Was that a fake wall?" I asked, moving beside him.

Before he could answer, a gray blur hissed by his boot—a squirrel, its tail puffed and furious. I jumped back as it shot toward the door. Bruno barked once and darted after it, determined to protect the barn from all intruders.

"Bruno!" I called, but before I could follow, Logan caught my arm. His voice dropped. "Didn't you say you found a bead here earlier today?"

I turned—and froze. Scattered across the dirt were shards of glass, seashells, broken marbles, and tiny white pearls glinting under the flashlight beam. The debris looked hauntingly familiar.

"They're like the jars from Arthur's office," I whispered.

Logan crouched, pulled on a latex glove, and brushed the hay aside. A few small, capped jars lay half-buried beneath the mess.

"Well," I said faintly, "that explains the teacups full of nails."

Logan looked at me with a clear, questioning expression. "People put hardware stuff in jars. But if they used them for—" I circled my hand above the mess. "For whatever this is, I guess they used the teacup to keep the nails in instead."

Logan didn't answer. He stood and angled the light higher—onto the exposed wall behind the wreckage.

For an instant, the beam caught something pale. Bone-white.

"Is that—"

Logan turned quickly, placing himself between me and the wall. "You don't want to see this one, Maggie."

My heart pounded. "What—who—"

He pulled out his phone and dialed. "I think you actually found Ruth," he said grimly. He stepped outside the stall and kept walking out of the barn while giving the address and requested a forensic team.

Bruno came bounding back into the barn, panting, tail wagging—but instead of running to me, he stood in front of the broken stall and barked sharply, over and over.

"Bruno, come on," I called softly, edging toward him. "You found her. Good boy. Let's go—"

He didn't move. His barks deepened, fo-

cused toward the far corner of the fake wall
—*not* where the skeleton was.

A chill ran through me.

I stepped carefully around the scattered jars
and crouched beside him. "What is it, boy?"

Bruno sniffed along the boards, then
stopped and barked twice at the same spot. I
recognized that look—he'd found something.

Grabbing a rake from near the pen, I used
it to pry at the wallboards. On the second
strike, the wood split, revealing a dark gap. I
tugged again, widening it, but the rake caught
on something solid behind it.

Holding my breath, I pulled the tool back.
The light from the desk lamp caught on black
fabric—something large, hidden, and far too
new to belong in an old barn. I hooked the rake
under the edge and pulled gently. The fabric
tore, and the unmistakable shimmer
of *money* spilled through the rip.

"Logan?"

He was already walking toward me, phone
still in hand. "Maggie, don't touch anything.
This is a crime scene now."

"Oh, I know. How would you like to add a
bag full of money to it?"

Logan stopped dead, exhaled hard, then

rubbed the back of his neck. "You have got to be kidding me."

He lifted his phone again. "I need a team checking a suspicious vehicle in the parking lot of City Hall."

Bruno sat at my side, tail still, eyes fixed on the torn bag—like he knew exactly what we'd just found.

Chapter 14

I sat on the back of Logan's truck, watching officers move in and out of the farm. The night was no longer quiet or dark; it flashed red and blue with police lights, harsh spotlights, and a sea of flashlights sweeping through the property.

Bruno lay beside me, his head resting on his paws, probably exhausted after doing his job. He'd found both the body and the bag of money. It could also be the chase he had with that squirrel, though.

"Nothing on the car," I overheard an officer tell Logan. "Someone rented it a week ago outside the state, but the contact information is all fake."

Logan frowned and thanked him before walking towards me.

"I don't know what concerns me more," Logan said, walking toward me with that half-smile that appeared only when he was too tired to argue. "That you were right to be scared of the barn... or that you're still afraid of the goats."

I frowned, crossing my arms. "I'm *not* afraid of the goats. I just don't like the legend about them."

"Well," he said, pointing toward the barn, "you kind of destroyed our town legend anyway."

"What? How?"

"You found Ruth. So now," he said, mock-serious, "why are the goats supposed to take people?"

I opened my mouth to argue, but Arthur's voice cut through before I could.

"This won't affect the legend," he said, glancing up from the clipboard in his hands. "It may actually improve it. Whoever that is— it isn't Ruth."

Logan straightened. "How can you be so sure?"

Arthur smiled—a bright, cheerful smile that felt almost out of place given the situation. "Because the skeleton belongs to a male. Hard to tell the age, of course, but judging by the bones, the clothing, and the environment, I'd estimate he's been down there at least a hundred years. Give or take."

A chill ran down my spine. The night suddenly felt colder, heavier. For a moment, I could've sworn someone was watching us. Bruno lifted his head and stared toward the line of trees, ears twitching. When he didn't move or growl, I forced myself to breathe. Probably just nerves... and the season.

"Was he murdered?" Logan asked.

Arthur flipped through his notes, his brow furrowing. "Too early to tell. I'll need more time to examine the remains and run tests."

"Maggie!" a voice called, and all three of us turned. Tricia jogged toward us, clipboard in one hand, ponytail coming loose.

"Thank goodness you're still here," she said, catching her breath. "I mean—I'm sorry you're *still* here, but I need to ask you something."

"What is it?"

"Do you still have that bead—the pearl you showed me earlier?"

I nodded and fished it from my pocket.

Tricia took it carefully and slipped it into a

plastic bag labeled *Evidence*. "You mentioned there's an arts and crafts classroom here, right?"

"Yes. Do you need to check it?"

She nodded. "That would be wonderful. Thank you—and sorry to keep you this late."

I looked at Logan, who leaned against the truck, arms crossed, smirking.

"No problem," I said. "My ride's still working the scene, so I guess I'm waiting anyway."

Bruno gave a quiet whine beside me, tail thumping once against the truck bed—as if to agree.

The farmhouse didn't have the same creepy feeling as the barn. Maybe it was the steady hum of the lights, or how every corner was bright enough to chase away shadows. Still, it felt strange seeing a whole team of officers combing through every room.

"Thanks for the help," Tricia said, snapping on a pair of latex gloves. "I'm sorry I didn't take your finding more seriously before. It just didn't match anything—at the time."

"What happened?" I asked, then immediately shook my head. "Never mind. You probably can't tell me."

A hand brushed my shoulder, and I nearly jumped. Logan.

"Ready to go?"

I wished Tricia luck and followed him outside. I wasn't expecting much conversation; he looked exhausted and distracted, the humor from earlier gone. So when he started answering the question I'd just asked *Tricia*, it took me a second to realize what he was saying.

"You never went up into the loft," he said, opening the car door for me after letting Bruno climb into the backseat. "The jars up there were half full, and there was a pile of weird dolls beside them. But the stuff around them looked... different. Even I could tell those weren't real pearls."

I buckled my seat belt and settled in. "I guess few people have an endless supply of expensive jewelry."

"Or antiques," he said. "Around a hundred years old."

"So the real question is—how does any of that connect to the bag of money?"

He glanced at me briefly before focusing back on the road. "You're going to figure it out anyway, so I might as well tell you. When we pulled down the rest of the boards, we found six more bags of cash. All small bills—ones, fives, a few tens. Not easy to trace, but definitely not something you forget hiding."

"And none of it was a century old?" I asked, which made him laugh—exactly what I wanted.

"What if they're not even related?"

He shook his head. "You're the one who always says there's no such thing as coincidence."

I shrugged. "Maybe not. But there *is* such a thing as a red herring."

He smirked. "That's for mystery books, Maggie. The police follow evidence."

Logan parked in front of my mom's house and came around to open my door, Bruno trotting beside him.

"I'm glad you asked me to go with you," he said quietly.

"Are you kidding? I wouldn't have set foot in that barn alone at night."

He chuckled, shaking his head. "I guess now there's no way I can convince you curses aren't real."

"For the record," I said, pointing at him, "I

don't believe in curses. I just don't *play* around with them. Just in case."

He smiled, but before he could leave, a thought struck me. "Do you think Tolbert and this suspect had some kind of—I don't know, side business or something?"

Logan turned back, hands in his pockets. "Side business? You mean like illegal business?"

I shrugged. "Money makes a big difference, no? Isn't that a motive?" I said, which made Logan frown at me.

"What? I'm just putting the evidence together."

He sighed. "Good night, Maggie."

"You should check Tolbert's bank accounts," I said as he walked pass me.

"See you tomorrow, Miss Willow."

"Good night, Detective."

I watched him walk back to his car, and only when I closed the door did I notice his headlights stayed on a moment longer than necessary. I wanted to think it was chivalry—but the thought of the suspect still out there crept back in.

If the money had been his motive, then finding it meant I'd just taken away everything he wanted.

Montie Red

A shiver crawled up my spine as I locked the top latch on my mom's front door, then checked the back. Bruno circled once by my feet before lying down, ears alert.

This case was getting too complicated.

Chapter 15

The next morning, I was about to step inside City Hall when someone whispered my name from behind a column.

"Maggie." Miss Tony's voice was low but sharp, commanding as ever.

She beckoned me toward the corner of the parking lot. Bruno, however, stopped short and pulled me back. He had planted himself in the exact spot where that strange car had been parked yesterday. My first thought was that he'd scented something important.

"What are you doing?" Miss Tony hissed, motioning urgently. "Come on!"

I tugged gently on the leash, but Bruno sat stubbornly, refusing to move. With a sigh, I loosened the strap and peeked around the corner myself.

Gertrude waddled across the path. Now I could see her better. Its brown-speckled feathers bouncing with each step. A neat white line circled its eyes like a delicate mask. She glanced sideways at me, unimpressed, before continuing toward the pond.

"She's adorable," I said. Even without experience with birds, I knew she wouldn't appreciate being chased or picked up.

"Isn't she?" Miss Tony's face softened, glowing with motherly pride. But then her expression hardened, and her gaze snapped back to me. "I'm worried about the goats."

That caught my attention. When we moved them last weekend, the goats had looked perfectly content in her yard. Honestly, I'd been more worried about her bushes than the animals.

"Are they sick? Or... sad?" I asked.

Miss Tony raised an eyebrow, as if I'd just suggested they'd gone out shopping. "No, sweetie. They look better than when they arrived. The problem is sending them back. After what we've learned about that barn's condition, how could you possibly return them to a place like that?"

It took me a second to process. "Why would I send them back? Unless... you don't want them in your yard—"

"Absolutely not!" she cut me off, her tone fierce. "Those goats can stay for the winter if necessary."

"The winter? Why would they—"

"The barn was destroyed yesterday!" she exclaimed. "It's all over town. The police tearing down walls, finding... well, you know. Whoever that poor soul was, may they rest in peace."

It never failed to amaze me how fast news traveled in Apple Creek. "Did Arthur tell you?"

Miss Tony's eyes narrowed. "Arthur would never divulge police matters. He's like his father was—secretive, professional."

I opened my mouth to apologize, but she forged on. "I have my own sources. I stay away from gossip, but certain things reach me anyway. So let's be clear—you are not taking those goats back."

"Not yet," I admitted. "We still have the festival coming."

Her frown deepened. She folded her arms. "You can't possibly be thinking of using that barn now. It's cursed!"

"Cursed?" I echoed.

She brushed her short hair back and squared her shoulders. "How else do you explain the shooting—just to stop the singer from performing—and now another dead body? It isn't coincidence."

"Maybe someone just really missed the goats?" I joked, though the look she gave me made me instantly regret it.

She stepped closer, lowering her voice. "That's what I thought too, at first. But then it hit me: what if it wasn't about the goats at all? Think about it—the singer would have brought attention to the barn. Stages, lights, speakers, people swarming everywhere. Too much risk. Just like the goats. Margaret, when was the last time anyone used that part of the barn? Whoever hid that body clearly wanted it kept shut away."

Her theory almost sounded logical... until she leaned in, gripped my hand, and pulled me close to whisper.

"And of course, we know whoever hid that body decades ago must be long dead. No one my age—or older—could be out here killing and outrunning the police." Her eyes glinted. "But a ghost could. That would explain the vanishing."

Bruno gave a sharp huff beside me, as if even he wasn't buying that explanation.

After promising Miss Tony that the barn would be repaired before the goats returned, she left for her office looking perfectly satisfied.

Me, on the other hand? I couldn't stop thinking about what she'd said. Not the part about the ghost—though the memory of feeling watched last night still crept up on me —but the rest.

Someone had wanted to keep that barn closed.

And I knew *two* people who'd worked very hard to get those goats out of there.

Logan was right: coincidences weren't good. Thelma and Rose had been tangled in every strange event so far.

"Margaret," Linda called from my door. "Your sister's here. She's in the parking lot but doesn't want to come in. Wants to know if you can meet her out there."

I stepped to the window. Sure enough, Sandie's car sat parked by the far edge, and there she was—bouncing on her heels, baby carrier strapped to her chest.

"Thanks, Linda," I said, already heading out.

As soon as I stepped outside, Sandie rushed toward me. "Maggie, I need your help."

"What happened? Is everyone—"

She shook her head, but her tense expression didn't ease my worry. "I had to do something," she said, kissing tiny Leslie's head and starting toward the back of the lot. "I owe him that much. He doesn't have family nearby, and I know Logan couldn't get involved."

I frowned, trying to catch up to both her stride and her logic. "Logan couldn't—? Are you talking about Henry?"

She nodded, bouncing slightly on her heels again. Poor Leslie's head bobbed with each movement, somehow still sound asleep.

"What did you do, Sandie?"

"I paid his bail."

I stopped cold. "You *what*?"

She bit her bottom lip, eyes glistening. "I don't have feelings for him, Maggie. I love Paul —probably more now than when we got married—but you asked about Henry, and then he showed up and..." She swallowed. "I felt guilty for how I left him. I just—had to do something."

"And paying his bail was your *something*?"

Sandie looked down, voice soft. "It's what he needed most right now, right?"

"Does Paul know?"

Her cheeks flushed. "Kind of."

"*Kind of*? How do you 'kind of' tell your husband you're paying another man's bail? Did you lie about who it was for?"

She shook her head, barely whispering. "No. I told him I needed to do something for Henry."

My mouth fell open, but before I could say anything, she continued, voice suddenly firm. "He knows everything, Maggie. From the beginning. Paul knew what happened between Henry and me. He's not happy I came, but... he understands."

I crossed my arms. "And what *did* happen between you two?"

Sandie sighed and looked skyward, like she wished the story would vanish into the clouds. "Long story short, Henry had our whole life planned out. Perfect, on paper. But I started realizing I didn't agree with his 'ideal future.' So when he proposed, I panicked."

"Panicked how?"

"I walked away. Literally. He was down on one knee, and I just... turned and left. I ran home, packed a bag, and took the first train out."

The image of poor Henry kneeling there wasn't hard to picture. "Did you ever talk to him afterward?"

She shook her head. "I didn't know what to say. I didn't even plan to meet Paul so soon. I just... left. Before Saturday, the last time I saw Henry was that night."

She kissed Leslie's forehead again. "Paul knows. He understood I needed to do this for Henry—as an apology."

Before I could answer, someone called my name from the entrance of City Hall. I didn't need to look to know it was Henry.

Sandie stiffened immediately, bouncing again as nerves took over.

"Maggie!" he shouted, jogging toward us. His hair was a mess, and his suit was in worse condition than it had been in the interrogation room. He stopped, cleared his throat, and looked at me. "You didn't have to do that, but I promise I'll pay you back. As soon as they unfreeze my accounts."

"It wasn't me," I said.

Sandie flushed bright red.

Henry's gaze turned to her—surprised, then quietly grateful. "Thank you," he said. "I'll pay you back."

She barely looked up. "I just hope they clear you soon, so there's no need."

Bruno gave a low huff beside me, sensing the awkward silence that fell over the parking lot.

I clapped my hands lightly. "So... what about lunch?"

Without waiting for an answer, I climbed in the passenger seat of my sister's car—because at that moment, it seemed like the safest place to be.

Chapter 16

I knew how small Apple Creek was, so we went to the ice cream shop instead of the bakery or pub. The last thing Sandie or Henry needed was the extra attention—and honestly, after everything, it felt like an *ice cream day* for everyone.

Mrs. O'Leary, the shop's owner, let us sit out on the patio even though the air had that crisp, end-of-season chill. She was probably ready to close for the year, but she didn't say a word.

"So, you're telling me you went looking for Mrs. Jacobson to get the job?" I asked.

Henry nodded, spoon in hand. "I told you before," he said, then hesitated when he caught Sandie's eyes. He dropped the spoon into his bowl and exhaled. "I got fired a few weeks ago

—maybe a month or so. Lost my apartment. Haven't found a new job yet."

He looked at my sister. "Logan offered to let me stay with him until I figured things out. I was desperate, saw the article about the weird break-in, and thought those women might need legal help. So, I reached out."

"And everything got complicated," Sandie said quietly. It was the first time she'd spoken since the parking lot. "How bad is it?"

Henry took a slow breath, his gaze fixed on his melting ice cream.

"Do you remember anything else?" I asked. "After we talked at the station?"

Sandie's head snapped toward me. "You talked to him at the—"

"That's not important," I interrupted, steering the conversation back before she could accuse me of meddling. "What about Bert? Anything new from him?"

Henry rubbed his forehead. "It doesn't look good. From what I've gathered, he's being charged with conspiracy to commit murder."

Sandie winced. "And they're charging *you* with the same?"

He nodded. "Though the police haven't found any real connection between Bert and me. And besides the case, I had no ties to Tolbert at all."

"So they don't have proof," Sandie said hopefully.

Henry didn't answer, but the silence said enough.

"They've got evidence," I said for him. "Gunpowder on his hands, his car showing up at every crime scene and a gun in it..." I hesitated before adding, "Henry, do you really believe Thelma's story about wanting to *protect* the farm?"

Both of them looked confused.

"She sold it to the city," I explained, "losing money because she wanted to preserve it. Do you think that was really her motive?"

"That sounds noble," Sandie said. "And she's been a victim in all this, remember."

Henry frowned thoughtfully. "I don't know. I try not to question my clients more than necessary. My job was to represent her, not investigate her."

I was about to press further when my phone buzzed.

"Sorry," I said, standing up. "Be right back."

As I stepped to the far end of the patio, I could feel Sandie's eyes following me—

pleading for me not to leave her alone with him. I gave her a quick smile before answering.

"Hi, Logan," I said. "If this is about Henry's bail, I promise it wasn't my idea."

"What? Hold that thought," he said. "I need your help first."

I straightened, turning slightly away from the table. "What's going on?"

"We need to talk to Walter Gray. You met with him?"

"Yes," I said. "The city's historian."

Logan sighed, the sound rough through the line. "After what we found at the farm, we need to trace the ownership back as far as possible. But Mr. Gray won't talk to anyone except the *current owner*."

"And since the city owns it..."

"Exactly," he said. His voice softened. "I wouldn't ask if I had time to get a court order, but every hour counts right now. He also asked for you specifically."

That caught me off guard.

"Well, I'm happy to help," I said. "When do you—"

"If you're not busy, can you meet me there now?"

I turned toward the patio. Henry was

staring into his bowl again; Sandie was rocking Leslie gently, avoiding his eyes. Guilt rolled off both of them. Maybe this was the moment they needed—to talk, to clear the air.

"I'm not at the office," I told Logan, "but I can meet you at the... flower shop."

"The flower shop?"

"It's right next to the ice cream place. See you soon."

I ended the call and called over to the table, loud enough for them both to hear. "I've got to help Logan with something! I'll see you at the house later."

Sandie looked like she was about to faint, but I smiled and added, "Henry, we'll figure this out, okay?"

Then I waved to Mrs. O'Leary, who was watching us from the counter with that knowing small-town smile that said *she already had her own version of this story.*

Bruno trotted beside me as I left the patio —leaving behind two people with a lot more to say to each other than they probably wanted to admit.

A tiny bell jingled above the door as I stepped inside, and the sweet aroma of flowers wrapped around me like a warm scarf. Buckets and vases lined the shop, each overflowing with colorful blooms. At the center table stood a massive fall arrangement—bursts of orange and yellow mixed with pinecones, acorns, and tall stems of dried wheat.

"Margaret Willow," came a familiar voice, "I certainly hope you didn't forget your mother's birthday."

I turned to see Mrs. Gladis Williams, owner of the flower shop—and one of the R-Parks Department's most loyal fans. Also, possibly the pickiest person in Apple Creek when it came to soil quality.

"Mrs. Williams," I said, smiling, "my mom's birthday is in January."

She tapped the edge of the table. "Exactly my point. That would be a very *long* and *very bad* forget, don't you think?"

I supposed she was right, but she didn't seem to need an answer. Instead, she crouched down to greet Bruno, who wagged his tail politely.

"This handsome boy's a keeper," she said. "I heard he's taking a few days off after that awful shooting."

She drifted toward the back of the shop, where a worktable overflowed with trimmed stems and curling ribbons.

"Yes," I said, following her, "he's been helping the R-Parks Department for a bit. Light duty."

Mrs. Williams raised a perfectly arched brow and pressed her lips together. "I wasn't going to say anything, Maggie, but since you're here—and since my dear friend Mary is *so* worried—" She leaned closer, glancing toward the front window. "You know Tolbert's house is by the golf course, right? Are you familiar with that lovely area?"

I nodded, bracing for what was surely going to be a delicate piece of *community intelligence*, also known as gossip.

"Anyway," she whispered, "Mary's husband is terribly upset. He's quite the golfer, you know, and he says the police spotlights over the course are *ruining* it. The weight of those big lamps is digging into the special area."

I frowned. "The special area?"

"Oh, you know—where you kick the ball into the hole. The inn-line?"

"The *green*?"

She snapped her fingers. "Yes! The green! He swears the ground will never recover. As

an *advanced gardener*, I completely understand. You may want to talk to the police about
moving those lights."

Before I could respond—or explain that I
was not, in fact, the Chief of Police—the bell
over the door jingled again.

"Well, if it isn't someone I *never* see in
here," Mrs. Williams said with a grin.

"Perfect timing," I muttered as Logan
stepped in.

He smiled at Mrs. Williams, but I hurried
over and grabbed his arm. "We're in a hurry,
Mrs. Williams. I'll check on Mary's green problem, promise."

"Mrs. Williams," Logan started politely,
but I was already steering him toward the door.

Of course, she couldn't let us leave quietly.

"Logan Forest!" she called after us, loud
enough to echo down Main Street. "I expect to
see you back here buying flowers for Maggie!
How's a couple supposed to have a healthy relationship if their bouquets are months apart?"

I didn't dare turn around. That was my
punishment for leaving my sister alone with
Henry—I'd pay for it in small-town embar-
rassment.

Logan, however, laughed and called something back to her that I didn't catch, because I was already holding the car door open for Bruno.

Chapter 17

Logan laughed when I finished explaining why he'd found me in the flower shop. At the time, it had seemed like a clever idea—but I knew Mrs. Williams, and I should've known better. There was a reason I didn't buy flowers often, even though my mom loved them.

"I appreciate the gesture," Logan said as he steered up the short hill toward the senior living facility. "It probably saved me an awkward run-in with Henry."

I opened my door once he parked. "You haven't talked to him?"

Logan shook his head, holding Bruno's leash as we walked toward the entrance. "I'm not his lawyer," he said with a wink.

"Me neither," I muttered, remembering my

conversation with Henry in the station. "Did you really point your gun at him?"

He didn't answer—just held the door for me. I took that as a yes.

At the front desk, a cheerful woman greeted us. Her smile widened when she saw Bruno.

"He's adorable," she whispered, then covered her mouth. "Sorry, I know he's an officer; otherwise, he wouldn't be able to be here. What can I do for you?"

"I was hoping to speak with Mr. Walter Gray. He may be expecting me—Margaret Willow, from the R-Parks Department."

She nodded, dialing quickly, and a moment later said, "He'll see you in his apartment. Do you know how to get there?"

Since neither of us did, she guided us through hallways that looked more like a hotel than a retirement home. When we reached the third floor, she gestured toward a door and excused herself.

I knocked, and a deep voice called, "Come in!" followed by the slow shuffle of footsteps.

Leaning on the wall, Logan smirked. "I'm glad we're not in a hurry."

The door opened to reveal Walter Gray,

wearing khaki Bermudas and a thick wool sweater.

"Margaret! So nice to see you again. Please, come in."

His apartment resembled a miniature library—walls lined with bookshelves, piles of volumes stacked in corners, even the bed in the adjoining room surrounded by teetering towers of hardcovers. The smell of old paper and ink filled the air, the kind of scent that makes book lovers weak in the knees.

"Walter," I said, motioning toward Logan. "This is Detective Logan Forest."

"Detective," Walter greeted warmly. "We spoke on the phone. I'm glad you managed to reach Miss Willow."

He lowered himself into an old leather chair by the window. "Please, sit. Whatever we accomplish here can happen standing or sitting, though I prefer the latter these days."

I took the chair nearest him, while Logan chose one farther back.

"I heard about the discovery of a body in the barn," Walter began, folding his hands. "I can't say I'm shocked. Given the history of that farm, it was bound to happen eventually."

Logan leaned forward, but I asked first.

"What history? The city archives only show the Jacobson family as the previous owners."

Walter frowned thoughtfully. "The Jacobsons? You mean that lady and her niece?"

"Yes. Thelma and Rose. She sold the farm to the city to protect it from being torn down for condos."

Walter chuckled softly. "Convenient, perhaps—but I think her motives were even more... personal."

He looked at Logan. "I've suspected this for years, but until now, I've never had proof that I was right."

Logan's expression tightened, his weariness turning to focus.

"All right," Walter said, glancing between us. "You know the legend of Ruth. I assume you're both old enough to have snuck out to the barn at night and waited to hear the goats cry?"

I was certain I imagined the slight shift in his tone—the one that made the air feel just a little colder.

"According to the city register," he continued, "Ruth married at fifteen to an older man, Thomas Deaport. He owned the farm, but also a mill in Maple Hollow and several city investments. Two years after their marriage, Thomas sailed for Europe and never returned. No one thought much of it—because around the same time, Ruth also disappeared, leaving the farm to her sister, Dorothy. That's where the family line continues."

"Deaport didn't have any other family?" Logan asked, his interest sharpening.

Walter nodded. "He did. Two brothers, Franklyn, who inherited the mill, and George, who took the investments—until he lost them a few years later. Curiously, none of them ever claimed the farm. And only a month after Thomas's death, Franklyn married Dorothy—who happened to be Ruth's exact age."

Logan arched a brow. "And Ruth didn't have a twin sister, did she?"

"Not that I've ever found," Walter said, a faint smile tugging at his lips. "And believe me, I looked."

I pressed a hand to my mouth. "You think Ruth and Franklyn killed Thomas?"

Walter shrugged slightly. "There are letters from Franklyn to George, mentioning Thomas's temper. Some say he got into a fight overseas and never made it home. Others..." He tapped his chin. "Well, others believed his fate was decided much closer to Apple Creek."

Logan frowned. "Why didn't anyone speak

up? Surely someone must have missed a wealthy businessman."

"Perhaps," Walter said, "but people prefer legends to scandal. A missing man, a grieving sister, a convenient twin—it was easier to believe the tale than dig up the truth."

"Until we found a body," I murmured.

Walter nodded gravely. "You asked me recently about the ownership of the farm."

"Yes."

"Well, finding Thomas's remains may change everything. When George lost his fortune, someone filed a claim against the farm in his name. Franklyn's good reputation won him the case—but if the truth comes out, that judgment may no longer stand. And if the man claiming to be the rightful owner is descended from George..."

He paused, looking directly at me. "...then he may indeed have a legitimate claim."

I sat quietly in Logan's car for a long moment, watching the reflection of the senior facility fade in the side mirror. Walter's words circled in my head like stubborn leaves caught in the wind. Someone had killed a man and hidden his body in that barn nearly a century ago. Thomas Deaport had vanished, Ruth had disappeared, and somehow their story had lived on as a ghost tale about goats and curses.

"They'd still have to prove Ruth or Franklyn committed murder," Logan said, breaking the silence. "And they'd have to prove the body belongs to Thomas Deaport—which won't be easy."

I frowned. "You mean because the records are too old?"

"Exactly. And even if it *is* Thomas, taking the farm from the city would be a long shot."

I leaned my head against the seat, exhaling. "I just keep thinking about poor Ruth. Half an hour ago she was a missing girl, and now she's possibly a murderer? Walter's theory makes sense, but how could anyone ever prove—or disprove—it?"

Logan smiled faintly. "Glad you asked."

I crossed my arms. "That sounds suspiciously like you already have a plan."

He pulled onto the road, eyes on the windshield. "We're going to see the only living relatives we know from that family."

I arched a brow. "We?"

"Unless you're too busy," he said casually. "I can drop you at City Hall."

Of course I had a mountain of work waiting—but there was no way I was missing this. "So, you need my help to talk to Thelma... or you're just afraid of her? You know, because of the goat curse and all."

He chuckled. "Maybe I just want to spend time with you."

I wasn't expecting that. And if he'd looked away from the road for even a second, he would've noticed the blush spreading across my cheeks.

"Or," he added, amusement tugging at his voice, "maybe I know you too well—and I'm certain you'd try to talk to Thelma and Rose on your own. So I'd rather be there when you do."

That sounded more like him. Still, I couldn't help smiling. "You can't deny I've been helpful in the past."

He glanced at me then, his expression turning serious. "Of course not. But I also can't forget how many times you've ended up in danger. As long as I can help it, I'll make sure you're safe."

I opened my mouth to protest, but he cut me off with a grin.

"And for the record," he said, "the one who's afraid of the curse isn't me—it's you."

Chapter 18

Logan pushed the door open when from inside we herd Thelma saying that we could walk in. The house was a small old wooden cottage, with small windows that kept the inside slightly on the dark side. It reminded me how I would picture Hansen and Gretel's or the little red hooded's grandmother house in the woods. Hopefully without the witch or the wolf inside.

Thelma was sitting by a table full with empty jars, beats, seashells and necklaces. In her hands, she was holding an old letter and among the stuff, I could see a pile of old letters, a very old wooden box with the letters R and D engraved on it.

"I can't believe she did it," Thelma said her eyes lost in the distance and her expression pale and in shock. "I thought I was protecting her. Not embarrassing her. I tried to explain the severity of our legacy and I thought..." she lifted her eyes and focused on Logan. "I don't even know where to start to apologize, detective."

Logan pointed at a chair and waited until she nodded to offer me a seat and then he sat down.

"What about you start with this?" He pointed at the stuff on the table. "Rose, I assume?"

Thelma's eyes closed and I noticed a few tears escaping her eyelids. I reached out and touched her hand. She looked at me and explained.

"I was going to clean her room and I found —" she pointed at the stuff on the table. "I confronted her. I was still hoping I got things wrong but she—apparently she wants to leave Apple Creek because I embarrassed her. My concern with the farm sound to her as an obsession and she had trouble making friends. But who wants to be friend with people that make fun of your family?"

Rose's point of view seemed understandable to me because of her age. Thelma could come across as intense and for teenagers probably as crazy too. I also could understand Thelma's position though. Kids could be mean and that didn't justify Rose's actions.

"Where did Rose get real pearls?" Logan asked.

Thelma sighed and looked at the table. "The farm. Our family had kept portions of Ruth's wealth hidden in there. Most of the fortune got lost over time. By the time my mother got a hold on the farm, there was nothing. The farm became a dead weight and..." she looked at me. "You know the reason I sold it. I couldn't keep it. It was just too expensive for me. Those pearls were more a memory than a financial value. Rose had seen them. I showed them to her plenty of time while she was growing up. I guess she decided to show me how much she hated my family. Me."

Her tone sounded sad and devastated. I could easily imagined myself fighting with Darcy and that idea broke my heart.

"I have to ask, Thelma," Logan said. "Did Rose kill—"

Thelma's hit hard hands against the table sending a few of the beats down. "No! She didn't hurt anyone. She wanted to scare me. To force us to move. I sold the farm and according to her, we had nothing to do here. But of course, I couldn't. I needed to make sure no one found—" she closed her eyes. "The body in the barn."

Logan nodded and leaned on the table. "Thomas Deaport?"

Thelma's face lost all color and she sat back, hiding her hands on her lap. "I don't know who—how do you know this?"

I was going to answer, but Logan talked first. "That isn't important. What matters is what you know. I'm listening."

She shook her head and shuffled on her seat, but after only a few seconds, she exhaled and pushed the pile of letters towards Logan.

"My mother gave me these before she passed. Those are the letters that Ruth and Franklyn sent to each other."

She looked at me. "It is just a sad love story. Franklyn fell in love with Ruth. Both were almost the same age, but Thomas was the one leading the Deaport's and wasn't going to let his younger brother marry before him. He forced Ruth's father into giving his daughter hand, and... well Thomas was a monster of a husband."

Thelma put intertwined her hands and stared at them. "Apparently it was an accident. Ruth was trying to run away and Thomas figured it out. He chased her into the barn. Ruth's goats?" She smiled at me. "Those were real. She feed them and care for them. I don't think they attacked Franklyn to defend Ruth, but when he jumped into their stalk in the middle of the night, well, those four weren't happy and one kick snapped the guy's neck."

The chill idea made me shivered, and I made a mental note to call Miss Tony and asked her to not scare those goats.

"It was a bizarre accident and well, back then being a woman was difficult. The constables wouldn't have believed Ruth's story and she would had ended up hanged or burned for witchcraft."

Logan sat back and crossed his arms. "Franklyn set up everything?"

Thelma nodded. "Without Thomas he was the head of the family, and no one questioned the Deaport's back then. It helped how most people disliked Thomas."

"So Ruth was really Dorothy and she ended up marrying Franklyn?" I asked.

Thelma nodded. "But only my family, and just the one inheriting the farm knew about this. How did you figure?"

"Our historian is a clever man," I sat forward and looked straight at her. "Which is the reason I need to ask. Is there anyway Tolbert could have been related to George Deaport? If he was, then the farm—"

"George didn't have a family," Thelma said and handed me the letter in her hand. "He died a few months after the wedding. He was a bad gambler and got attacked on an alley. I wanted to make sure this was truth so... well here is the one that Franklyn wrote to Ruth about it."

Logan cleared his throat. "How do I know you didn't forge this—"

Suddenly, a door down the small hallway opened. Logan stood up, hand already reaching for his gun, but when Rose started to shout he just stepped back and listen.

"My aunt didn't hurt anyone! It was me who filled the jars and put the stupid doll on the table. I did it."

Logan didn't have to raise his voice for everyone in the room to feel the pressure. His calm was sharper than anger.

"You saw Billy Tolbert before he got killed?" he asked.

"No, I didn't!" Rose said, looking at her

aunt with trembling hands and tears in her eyes. "I saw a man outside the barn, but not Billy Tolbert. I never met him."

"So, tell me what happened," Logan said, unmoved by her tears or fear.

Rose's fingers twisted in her lap. "I—I didn't mean to get anyone in trouble. I just—"

Her aunt, Thelma, cut in. "Detective, my niece has been terrified since all this started. I told her to be honest, but please remember she's just a girl."

Logan leaned forward, elbows on his knees. "Then let's start simple. You just told me you saw a man. What exactly did you see?"

Rose hesitated. "It was still dark, early morning. I'd gone back to check the jars I left in the barn after the school group came. I didn't want anyone tripping on the beads."

I exchanged a look with Logan. I had been correct before. She wasn't supposed to be volunteering at the farm over the weekends, and the fact that she lied about it bothered me.

"I locked the doors of the barn," she continued, "but forgot something in the farmhouse so I went back, and that's when I saw him. He was trying to break in."

"Did he see you?" I asked gently.

Rose shook her head. "No. He just kicked

the door, then went back to his car and drove off toward the field. I didn't recognize him—it was too dark—but when I saw the news later, I figured he was the one who killed Billy Tolbert."

Logan frowned. "Because he tried to break into the barn?"

Rose nodded quickly, too quickly. "No—yes..." she looked at Thelma and bit her lip bottom lip. "Sorry... I heard my aunt over the phone with that lawyer. Tolbert was suing the city for the ownership of the barn. I realized the pearls... there were valuable, and I figured he might need money. I thought the guy had been Billy himself until I heard in the news he got killed."

Logan showed Rose his phone, "is this the car?"

She nodded. "It was clean when he drove off, though."

Thelma's hand came down on her niece's shoulder, too firmly to be comforting. "She was upset about my behavior, about the goats and about the farm. She didn't mean to intrude in the farm or the police investigation."

I caught the slip in her voice—the one that meant she'd been rehearsing this part. "You knew the lawsuit was against the city,

why did you agree to meet with Mr. Klauer?"
I asked.

Thelma's mouth tightened. "Mr. Klauer contacted me after the article in the paper. He thought we needed help with the vandalism. I asked him to check it out," she smiled at her niece. "I didn't know then it was just Rose." Her tone hardened. "Mr. Klauer is the one who discovered the lawsuit and asked me to talk to him about the sale and my family history. As you should know, I want the farm to be preserved, so I agree to talk to him."

"And what did you tell him?" Logan asked, his tone neutral.

Thelma nodded. "Not much. On Saturday, I still believed my family's secret was protected. I just showed him a few letters, the deeds, the sale contract. He was polite... kind, even. I didn't expect any of this."

Logan looked at her carefully. "The letters you mentioned—where are they from?"

"They belonged to my great-great-grandmother, Dorothy Deaport," Thelma said. "They prove the man you found in the barn was Thomas Deaport, Ruth's husband. His death has been in our family stories for generations."

"Family stories," Logan repeated, skeptical.

"They were real people, Detective," she said, defensive now. "And if you look at those letters, you'll see how it was all an accident. I'm the last Deaport's descendent. George had no family, so there is no one besides Rose who could have inherited the farm or anything on it."

That last line lingered too long in the air.

Logan finally nodded. "We'll need to see those letters."

"Of course," Thelma said quickly. "Anything to help."

Rose stayed quiet, but her eyes darted between us, full of guilt. When Logan stood, she flinched.

"You'll both need to come to the station," he said, calm again. "We'll take formal statements there."

Thelma nodded, but her voice wavered. "Is that really necessary?"

"It'll clear things up," I said.

When we stepped outside, the cool air felt like a relief. I waited until we reached Logan's car before I spoke. "Something's off, isn't it?"

He didn't answer right away, just let Bruno climb into the backseat. "Family stories. Old lover letters. A century old body they had kept quiet for generations." He closed the door. "Yeah, something's off."

I folded my arms. "You think Rose lied about the barn?"

Logan started the engine. "I think she saw something. Just not what she said. And Thelma's too calm for a woman who just lost a fortune by her niece's prank."

"I know Henry reached out to her," I said. "But if she truly cares to preserve the farm, why didn't she reach out to the city about the lawsuit? That was going to be on us, not her."

He nodded slowly. "Exactly."

Bruno let out a low huff from the back seat. I agreed with him completely.

Chapter 19

Thelma and Rose arrived at the police station, where Logan and Bruno had been waiting for them. My sweet Bruno trotted between them, tail swishing proudly as if he were escorting two important witnesses. I stayed back to give Martin a quick summary — the jars, the lawsuit, and Thelma's family story.

Martin agreed it sounded like a civil matter more than a criminal one, but he still wanted to run everything by the city lawyer and the Mayor. To me, it felt like the real mystery was still hidden in that barn. Neither Thelma nor Rose had mentioned the bags of money, and if that wasn't suspicious, I didn't know what was.

I was just turning the corner toward the elevator when I caught voices down the hall.

"Mom, we can't talk about this."

Arthur stood there, hands buried in his hair, while Miss Tony lectured him with both hands on her hips. Bruno, curious, perked up beside me and gave a soft huff — his version of *you might want to see this.*

"Why not?" she fired back. "It's in the newspaper! And if I know anything, Arthur Lawrence Cooper, it's when not to discuss an open case with an officer. Which, I'll remind you, you are not."

Arthur groaned, rubbing his temple. Bruno let out a quiet whine, as if sympathizing.

Before I could retreat, Miss Tony spotted us. "Margaret!"

So much for escaping. Bruno's tail stopped mid-wag, like even he knew we'd just been caught.

"You should know this too," she said, marching over. "It's my understanding you've been doing your own police investigating again."

Bruno gave a sharp bark at the word *police*, tail wagging hard. Miss Tony bent down to rub his ears. "Oh, you're much better company than your human officer partner, you know that?"

I opened my mouth to deny the "investigating" part, but she was already off and running.

"If the newspaper says witnesses placed that singer — Billy Tolbert — in Apple Creek earlier this winter, how is it breaking any rule for me to ask whether the police confirmed it?"

"Wait," I said. "What do you mean Tolbert was here in winter?"

Miss Tony straightened, eyes wide with importance. "Well, according to the article, his neighbor said the house wasn't empty all year like everyone thought. Apparently, he was here in January, talking about retirement and—get this—a *family fortune.*"

"A family fortune?"

"Yes! Sounded ridiculous to me too, but money makes people do horrible things." She tilted her head down to Bruno. "Right, handsome? You know what greed smells like, don't you?"

Bruno sneezed, which only made her more delighted.

"Mom," Arthur groaned, "you can't just repeat everything you read. Those articles twist things to sound dramatic."

"Was Billy Tolbert murdered?" she asked.

Arthur hesitated. "Yes, but—"

"Well, then it's important to know if any of

that information's been confirmed, right, Margaret?"

I glanced at Arthur, who shook his head so hard I thought his glasses would fly off. "It's worth asking," I admitted carefully. "If Tolbert was looking for an inheritance or old family money, it would explain why he was so interested in the farm."

Arthur groaned again. "Please don't encourage her. The last time she got on one of her theories, she called the Mayor about alien signals near the radio tower."

Miss Tony ignored him completely. "Have the police questioned that other man—what's his name? Bert Smith? They went to school together. If Billy was hunting for a hidden fortune, Bert might've known about it."

That wasn't a bad thought, actually. I knew Bert wasn't close to Tolbert because of the emails, but back in high school, maybe they had been. I needed to know why Tolbert was so interested in the farm. Obviously, it could be the bags of money, but the pearls were valuable too—and there was still the body in the barn. It was odd that using the barn for the concert had been *his* idea.

"Miss Tony," I said, "do you happen to

know if there are any old high school yearbooks from when Billy went here?"

Her eyes lit up instantly. "Brilliant! I know exactly where to find them. I'll bring them to your office later today."

Bruno wagged his tail as she pushed the elevator button, and the doors opened immediately.

"See?" she said, smiling at him. "Even the building agrees I'm onto something."

The doors closed before Arthur could protest. He threw his hands in the air. "Maggie, please! Don't encourage her. She already thinks she solved half my dad's cases."

I chuckled. "I didn't know your dad was a police officer."

Arthur sighed. "He wasn't—FBI, actually. And Mom's been retelling his adventures ever since. That's why I stopped mentioning my family to anyone."

Bruno gave a small snort, like he found that hard to believe.

Arthur pointed at me, mimicking his mom's habit. "I mean it, Maggie. She'll have the kitchen wall covered in red yarn before dinner."

"But... she mentioned how it was more likely

that someone wanted to keep the goats *out* of the farm to hide something—before we found the body." I shrugged. "That sounds right to me."

Arthur frowned and, just like his mom, pointed a finger at me as he walked toward the station. "Don't encourage her, Maggie."

Bruno's tail thumped once, hard enough to echo down the hallway.

"You heard him, partner. No more encouraging Miss Tony."

He gave a small "boof" that I swore sounded like laughter.

After talking with my sister for over forty minutes, she seemed genuinely thankful for the chance to talk to Henry. I was even more surprised to learn he'd been invited to dinner at my mom's house. I didn't want to ask how that was going to go with Ben. Still, Sandie was happy, and Henry was out of jail — small victories, I supposed.

Bruno lay stretched beside my chair, one paw over his nose, sighing like he'd been the one doing the talking. His tail thumped lazily when I reached down to scratch behind his ears.

I wished I had better news about Bert. But aside from the emails, no one had found anything that could help him. Apparently, the judge wasn't convinced he hadn't known something, and the message Sophie showed me didn't exactly help his case.

"Margaret," Linda said from her desk, pointing at her phone. "Norman wants to talk to you. The smart guy still doesn't know your extension — and he's only worked here for, what, a year?"

Bruno perked up at the sound of Norman's name, as if expecting a treat delivery, and then flopped back down with a grunt. I laughed and picked up the call.

"Hello, Norman. How's it going?"

"Well, it'd be better if our Facilities Director was back at work instead of me taking over his load."

I felt a pang of guilt. Norman already had his hands full with Operations Maintenance, but I needed the help. Bert's position covered a lot of ground, and while we figured out what was going to happen to him, Norman took the parks, and I handled the buildings.

"Hopefully Bert will get cleared soon," I

said, "and then we can give him part of *your* job for a week."

Norman laughed. "I just hope he gets out of there soon."

"Me too. But how can I help you?"

"Right!" I heard an engine turn on and then a car door slam. "I finished going over the park reports for the week. Aside from a swing that needs replacement — looks like a non-infant tried to use it — and a few logs that need swapping in the nature playground, everything looks good."

At least the parks were running smoothly. Those small issues were normal for high-use areas. "That's great. I'll fill out the paperwork to get them replaced as soon as possible. Hey, maybe you should make rounds more often."

"Very funny, Margaret. You know the problem's the staff budget—oh, shoot. I almost forgot. We're missing a kayak."

Bruno lifted his head at the word *kayak*, ears twitching. He loved the river trails.

"A kayak?" I asked.

"Yeah, one of the ones we rent down by the river," Norman said, with zero concern. "It's not a big deal. People rent them, get tired before they reach the next dock, and leave them somewhere along the shore. They usually turn up by the bridge, or the city calls when one floats close to the dam."

That didn't sound great to me, but if Norman wasn't worried — and Bert had never mentioned it as a problem before — I figured it wasn't worth panicking about. Bruno gave a quiet *woof* under his breath, as if disagreeing.

"All right. Well, let me know when it shows up. Now you've made me curious."

"Will do."

He hung up, and though something about the missing kayak bothered me, I didn't have time to dwell on it. Bruno rested his chin on my foot, warm and steady — his subtle way of telling me to stop overthinking.

Just then, Miss Tony swept into the department, waving cheerfully before stopping at Linda's desk. Under one arm she carried a precarious stack of five large hardcover yearbooks. Bruno trotted to the doorway to greet her, tail wagging like a metronome.

"Well, hello there, Officer Bruno," she said, rubbing his head. "I brought evidence for your investigation."

He gave a proud little "boof," then padded back to his spot by my chair as she entered my office.

Chapter 20

I didn't expect Miss Tony to stay with me while I went over the yearbooks, but it ended up being surprisingly helpful. Bruno settled under the table between us, his chin on his paws, tail sweeping every so often against the carpet whenever someone laughed.

Linda, Sophie, and I had a blast listening to Miss Tony's commentary about school events from years ago — she told them as if they'd happened just this summer.

"I'm telling you," Miss Tony said, tapping a glossy photo, "we lost so many good teachers with this generation. These kids didn't have any sense of care for their grades — just party after party. Nothing like Margaret's generation."

I smiled and took the compliment. I didn't mention it was also her son's generation; I doubted she'd judge *him* as harshly as the others. Bruno's tail flicked once, like he agreed to keep that secret between us.

"How can you remember all that?" Sophie asked.

Miss Tony's expression brightened with pride. She straightened up, her tone full of theatrical gravity. "I've been blessed — and cursed — with an excellent memory. Faces, names, even what everyone wore to graduation. I just can't remember numbers. I can tell you all about the year, but never which one it was."

Sophie laughed, clearly impressed. Bruno stretched and gave a low sigh, the kind that rattled his jowls, which only made Linda giggle harder.

I couldn't imagine remembering things the way Miss Tony did. I was proud of myself when I could find Darcy's shoes in under ten minutes. Names and faces like she recalled them were beyond my abilities. Honestly, maybe *she* should be the one writing for the town paper instead of reading it.

My phone rang, breaking our rhythm. Bruno lifted his head, ears twitching as I reached for it.

"This is Margaret Willow."

"Margaret Willow — that sounds so formal." I recognized Francis's cheerful voice. "Are you too busy? I want to go over a few vendor details for the festival."

I looked at the ladies around the table. "Not too busy," I said, reaching for the file drawer. Bruno rose too, bumping my knee with his nose as if volunteering to help.

I didn't even have to say anything to Linda; she nodded, nudged Sophie toward the door, and mouthed *good luck* on her way out.

"Thanks, Margaret," Francis continued. "As you can imagine, some of our vendors are still nervous about everything that's happened in Apple Creek this week. I just want to reassure them their placements are far away from any, well, crime-related areas."

Miss Tony stacked the yearbooks neatly, gave Bruno one last affectionate pat, and whispered, "Keep an eye on her for me, Officer." He gave a polite little *woof* that made her beam before she left, closing the door gently behind her.

From the window, I watched the three of them still laughing together outside while I talked to Francis. I could practically hear Miss

Tony retelling some story about prom decorations gone wrong.

Francis's questions were reasonable — but also slightly exhausting. Yes, we'd have extra security. No, no one expected to dig up a century-old skeleton again. Bruno lay on his side, rolling just enough to bump the base of my chair, probably sensing my patience thinning.

"Do you think it would be all right if we met this Friday, Margaret?" Francis asked after nearly an hour on the phone. "That way I can collect everyone's concerns and go over them with you in person. Easier that way, don't you think?"

I guessed it made sense. Talking in person usually was easier, even if I still had half a festival to pull together. He must've caught my hesitation, because he added quickly,

"I'm happy to meet at the farm if that's easier. I don't want to interrupt setup."

"Thanks, that should help. Do you prefer morning or afternoon?"

"What about early morning? That way I can get back to work before noon."

I jotted the time and day into my planner. Bruno stood and stretched beside me, tail brushing my leg, as if approving the schedule.

"Early it is," I said.

By the time I hung up, the office felt quiet again — the kind of peaceful lull that comes after too much conversation. Bruno padded over, dropped his head in my lap, and let out a satisfied sigh. The festival might finally be coming together. One less problem, at least.

Chapter 21

My mom had asked me to stop by the ice cream shop to pick up dessert for dinner. The late afternoon air had that crisp edge that hinted fall was settling in, and for once, Bruno wasn't trotting at my side.

It was strange walking alone — no jingling collar, no huff of breath, no soft paws against the sidewalk. Logan had called my office soon after I finished talking to Francis and asked to keep him for the rest of the day. Apparently, they were running another sweep of the farm, and Bruno was needed there. I told myself it was routine, but a knot tightened in my chest all the same.

"Maggie!" Mrs. O'Leary called as soon as I opened the shop door. The scent of vanilla and waffle cones wrapped around me like comfort. "I have your mom's order ready." She leaned forward with that mischievous grin that always meant gossip. "I wasn't sure about your early meeting, but I have to say—it all worked out well."

I frowned. "What do you mean?"

Mrs. O'Leary planted both hands on her hips. "You leaving Henry and Sandie here!"

It felt like a lifetime ago — though it had only been days since that awkward morning. "Right. That was... honestly an accident. I didn't plan anything beyond meeting here."

"Well," she said, wagging a finger at me, "I had my doubts because Paul's a wonderful man, and for a moment I was worried. But seeing your sister and Henry talk—oh, it was good for them. The past can weigh you down if you don't let it out."

I nodded while paying for the ice cream. "You're probably right."

Mrs. O'Leary lowered her voice, eyes gleaming. "And I noticed you ducking into the flower shop, young lady. Is Logan all right? I can't imagine what it's like seeing his best friend in such a pickle."

I sighed. "He says he's fine, and Henry's staying with him while things get sorted out.

But honestly? I don't see how he *could* be fine. He hides it well, but..." I shrugged. "That's a lot to handle."

Mrs. O'Leary patted my hand. "Well, I'm glad he has you now."

I looked up sharply, cheeks warming. She smiled wider.

"I mean as a *friend*, Maggie."

I didn't get the chance to answer, because she changed the subject before my face cooled.

"I hate to bother you," she said, "but Larry's worried about the golf course."

"Larry?" I blinked, trying to catch up. "Is Patt Potter bothering him again? I thought since the golf course is closed for the season, the manager just ran out of there."

Mrs. O'Leary chuckled and shook her head. "Not Patt. But because he isn't there, Larry's getting a flood of complaints about some kind of police equipment out there — heavy lights or something like that."

I exhaled. "Yes, Mrs. Williams told me about that too. Her friend lives nearby and said the police lights are ruining the green."

Mrs. O'Leary nodded, relieved I already knew. "Larry's never been good with complaints. It keeps him up at night."

"I'll check it first thing in the morning," I

promised. "Tell him to relax — I'll make sure everything's all right."

She sighed in gratitude and handed me the bag of pints. I was about to leave when she stopped me with one last, pointed comment.

"And Maggie," she said, lowering her voice, "maybe you should sit down and *really* talk to Logan. You two have been dancing around each other for too long. Mrs. Williams and I are worried."

I blinked. "Worried?"

"That you'll run out of excuses before you realize you belong on the same team." Her grin softened into something almost maternal. "And you need more flowers, sweet lady. Flowers fix everything."

I laughed, though my cheeks were still burning. Outside, I paused by the car and glanced at the empty passenger seat. Normally Bruno would've been sitting there, ears perked, nose pressed to the glass.

Now the silence felt too big. I tightened my grip on the ice cream bag. "Stay safe, partner," I murmured.

A train whistle echoed faintly in the distance — the same haunting note that had followed the night they found the body.

And just like that, the knot in my chest pulled tighter.

The moment I opened my mom's front door, the sound of laughter rolled through the hallway — the kind that made the whole house feel alive again.

"Mommy!" Darcy shouted, barreling toward me in a pink tutu skirt and a pirate hat. "Everyone is here!"

"Everyone?" I scooped her up and spun her once. Her giggle filled the room, instantly fixing a day that had been far too long already.

When I set her down, she kept bouncing, chanting names like a proud little host. "Yes, everyone! Leslie and Toby and Aunt Sandie and Uncle Paul, and Grandma and Grandpa Ben, and a man named Henry — he's a lawyer!"

"What about Bruno?" I asked automatically. For a second, my heart lurched — had I misunderstood Logan and forgotten to pick him up?

Darcy stopped twirling. "Grandma sent him away."

"Sent him away?"

I followed her to the kitchen, where the smell of roast chicken and herbs wrapped around me like home. My mom stood by the stove, spoon in hand, while Ben helped her set the table.

"He was a mess!" my mom said, shaking her head. "There was no way I was letting him track all that dirt in here. That mud gets everywhere! I told Logan to keep him — or clean him — before setting foot in this house."

Ben chuckled. "You should've seen his face, Maggie. Looked like he'd wrestled a swamp."

"Mom," I groaned, "do you know how many groomers are open at this time of night?"

Sandie strolled in with Leslie on her hip. "And you need an appointment for those anyway."

I pointed at her but kept my eyes on Mom. "Did you hear that? You could've just let me wash him here."

"He can clean Bruno at his house," Mom said firmly, as if that settled it.

I muttered something about betrayal under my breath. Bruno would've loved the chaos here — he always stationed himself near Darcy's chair like the unofficial cleanup crew. The kitchen felt too quiet without the tap-tap of his paws on the tile.

"Logan said he'll bring Bruno later," Sandie added, cuddling Leslie. "He's coming to pick up Henry after dinner. Don't worry — you'll see him soon."

I frowned and took Leslie from her. "You hear that, little one? Your aunt thinks she knows everything. Maybe she shouldn't get ice cream tonight for being so naughty this morning." I grinned at Sandie. "Remind me again who's having dinner with us and why?"

Sandie crossed her arms, arching a brow. "You should fear revenge, Maggie."

"I thought you said it went well. Mrs. O'Leary confirmed it."

Sandie rolled her eyes. "Of course she did — that woman's a chronic romantic. And yes, all's good. It was nice to clear things up but..." She leaned close to whisper, "Don't say I didn't warn you. One day, you'll pay for the setup."

I mimicked her eye roll, though a tiny part of me believed her. My sister never let go of anything easily.

After dinner, Paul surprised everyone by heading to the basement with Henry to watch some kind of game. Mom took Toby and Darcy off to play while Leslie slept, leaving Ben, Sandie, and me to tackle the dishes.

"I'm sorry, Ben," Sandie said quietly, lowering her voice. "But is Maggie in any danger now?"

I froze mid-scrub.

Ben looked up from the dishwasher and gave us both a measured glance. "As far as I know, no. But if you know something, Sandie, you'd better tell me."

She shook her head, brushing hair from her face. "I don't. It's just... after what happened to Henry, I can't stop thinking. He'd never kill anyone — never. If he was framed, what's stopping this person from hurting Maggie next? She's the one who found the body, and the..." She hesitated, searching for the word. "The inheritance."

Ben straightened, all focus now. "What inheritance?"

"The farm," Sandie said. "Isn't this all about that place? Tolbert tried to claim it and ended up dead. The city owns it, but Maggie's the one running it. If someone covered up a murder for that long and now it's exposed... wouldn't they want revenge?"

Ben's expression hardened for a heartbeat, then softened again. "I don't think revenge is the motive."

"But what if—"

"Everything your sister's done, I've kept track of," Ben cut in, his tone gentle but firm. "And believe me, it's been the bare minimum necessary. Logan's on a very short leash with this case. There are things I can't tell you, but if I thought for one second Maggie was in danger..." He looked at me and smiled faintly. "I'd have her on house arrest myself just to keep her safe."

I opened my mouth to protest, but Darcy raced in, dragging a bag of blocks. "Mommy! We need Ben. He has to help build the castle!"

Ben laughed, drying his hands. "See? I'm reassigned." He followed her out, leaving soap bubbles and my protest behind.

"Well, that makes me feel better," Sandie said.

I grinned at her. "Then you're officially my accomplice."

Chapter 22

I was sitting on the porch swing at my mom's house, the air still warm but touched by the promise of fall. Darcy sat beside me, legs swinging, a half-eaten cookie in her hand. She'd been talking nonstop about school — new friends, a glitter project, and how the cafeteria chicken nuggets "weren't real." It was a wonderful change from crime scenes and city meetings.

Then she stopped mid-sentence and turned to me, her eyes wide with curiosity.

"Mommy, was Ben Grandma's boyfriend in high school?"

I laughed and shook my head. "No, sweetheart."

"What about Grandpa? You know — your dad in heaven?"

It caught me off guard. Darcy didn't often ask about my dad; she'd never met him, and we usually only mentioned him in passing.

"I don't think so, sunflower. I believe Grandma met him after high school."

She nodded thoughtfully, leaning against the pillows again, then popped upright. "What about you and Daddy?"

I narrowed my eyes, half-wary, half-amused. "Your dad and I met in college."

"Right. And we never married him."

I chuckled. "You're not wrong. Why do I feel like you're up to something?"

Darcy grinned — that mischievous, planning-something grin. "Nothing! I was just thinking... if Aunt Sandie didn't marry Henry but Uncle Paul, and Lucy didn't marry Logan but Jonathan, then maybe Grandma could marry Ben."

"Because she didn't meet him in high school?"

"Exactly!" Darcy clapped her hands. "But Grandma didn't like it when I told Ben that."

I bit back a laugh. "You told Ben he could marry Grandma?"

Her little shoulders hunched. "He laughed, but Grandma wasn't happy. I was serious,

Mommy. If they got married, Ben could live here with us."

I wrapped an arm around her. "I'm sure Grandma's not mad, pretty. But you can't ask adults to marry each other. That's something they decide on their own."

Darcy frowned. "So I can't ask Logan to marry us?"

My heart stuttered — partly from panic, partly from disbelief. I took a steadying breath and answered as calmly as possible.

"I don't think you can ask Logan that, sunflower. You have to know someone very well first — date them, build a relationship. Marriage is a big decision."

Darcy sighed dramatically. "Well, I don't want to marry Daddy anyway. He lives too far away. And did you know Australia is full of huge, poisonous spiders? I'm petrified of spiders!"

Footsteps crunched on the path before I could answer. Then a familiar tail wagged into view.

"Bruno!" Darcy squealed. She leaped off the swing and hugged him around the neck. His fur gleamed, freshly brushed, and he smelled faintly of soap and cedar-wood.

"You look so handsome! And you smell so

nice," she said, scratching his ears. "I missed you!"

Logan followed a moment later, leaning against the porch post. "Who's petrified of spiders?"

Darcy peeked up from behind Bruno's floppy ears. "Me! They're creepy — especially in Australia!"

"Are you going to Australia?" he asked, looking straight at me.

I shook my head quickly. "Nope. Staying firmly on this side of the ocean."

Darcy stood, tugging Bruno toward the door. "I'm giving Bruno a treat, Mommy! He's so clean, he deserves one."

"What about me?" Logan called after her, but the screen door slammed before he finished.

He gestured toward the door. "Can you believe that? I do all the work, and he gets the treats."

I smiled. "I can't believe my mom made you wash him."

Logan shrugged, running a hand through his damp hair. "In defense of your mom, he was a mess. I was too. We were crawling around under the barn for hours."

I blinked. "Under the barn?"

He nodded but didn't meet my eyes, tugging lightly at his sleeve like he regretted mentioning it. "Yeah. The team wanted to check something beneath the foundation. Turns out there's a crawl space we didn't know about."

"What did you find?"

He hesitated just a second too long, which told me plenty. "You know I can't tell you that, Maggie."

I crossed my arms. "That's not fair. You mentioned something about a secret space, finding something on it, and expect me not to ask questions?"

Logan's mouth curved in a faint smile. "You asking questions is exactly what Ben told me to watch out for."

I narrowed my eyes at him, half teasing, half suspicious. "So Ben *is* forcing you to keep an eye on me?"

He sighed, leaning forward on his knees. "He told me to keep you safe, and to keep you out of the case as much as possible. But Maggie..." He looked up then, his voice softer. "More than anything, your safety is my priority."

He reached out and brushed a strand of hair from my face, his fingers grazing my cheek. My breath caught.

"You're my priority," he said quietly.

My heart might've stopped — or raced too fast to tell the difference. He moved closer, the swing swaying slightly between us.

And, naturally, that's when the door opened.

"Thanks again," Henry said, stepping onto the porch with Ben right behind him. "Please tell Lucretia the food was delicious."

"Will do," Ben replied, smiling faintly before his gaze landed on us — on how close we were sitting. His expression darkened just a shade.

Henry gave me a warm nod. "Thanks, Maggie."

Logan stood, hands sliding into his pockets, expression unreadable. "Night, Chief." He gave me a quick half-smile before walking down the steps.

"Those two," Ben muttered, shaking his head. "I hope Henry really is as good as your mom and Sandie claim. I don't like having a suspect staying with one of my detectives."

I opened my mouth to respond, but Ben held the door open, that wry little smirk on his face.

"Come on, Maggie. Let's get inside before Darcy gives all the ice cream to Bruno."

Chapter 23

Too early in the morning for any reasonable person, Bruno and I walked into the country club. The building was half asleep — quiet, echoing, with only the faint scent of coffee and lemon cleaner in the air. The golf course had officially closed at the start of the month, and Patt had vanished south for "prestige-building" tournaments. Personally, I called it what it was: avoiding work.

"Boss!" Felix Collingwood, Mr. Elliot's nephew, called from across the lobby. His voice bounced off the empty space. "Larry said you might be coming, but not this early."

I grinned. "Didn't Logan tell you restaurant people start their days at dawn?"

Felix laughed, shaking his head as he jogged

over. "He also said we should have coffee ready for you in emergencies—but this counts as a surprise attack."

Bruno wagged his tail like he agreed with that assessment. I gave Felix a mock glare. "No worries. Bruno and I have a full day ahead. Why don't you tell me about these mysterious complaints?"

He nodded and led me toward the kitchen, where Larry O'Leary was already busy prepping breakfast for the staff. The smell of butter and fresh herbs made my stomach rumble.

"Morning, boss," Larry said with a grin. "Mom told me you'd stop by, but I didn't think you'd beat sunrise."

"I'm going to start thinking the two of you are hiding something," I said, hands on hips. Bruno gave a quiet *woof* like he seconded that suspicion.

Larry chuckled and waved his spatula. "Nothing like that. We just figured you'd want your coffee first before storming the greens."

I didn't tell them I knew the real reason for their nerves — the *Mayor's secret breakfasts*. Rumor had it that Mayor Dosal came here early every morning, pretending it was "club business," though everyone knew it was to escape his wife's cooking.

"Don't worry about the coffee," I said, "Mrs. O'Leary and Mrs. Williams both mentioned some neighbor worried about a spotlight ruining the green?"

Larry set down his knife and nodded. "That'd be the couple living next to the singer's place. They came in Sunday morning — said the police floodlights were still on the green near their house."

Felix added, "I checked right after that. All the spotlights were on the fairway, not the green. That's why we didn't bother you. I figured the police had already moved them."

"But," Larry continued, "about two days ago, last night and the night before, a few dinner guests told us one light was still out there, shining right on the grass. We checked every morning, and the spotlights were always on the fairway, not the green. Today we haven't had a chance to go see."

I sighed. "And this morning I show up before you have a chance to check."

They both nodded guiltily.

"Guys, this isn't your job," I said. "You're running the restaurant, and doing it well. Neighbors will always find something to complain about—especially with Patt gone." Bruno gave a small grunt, like even *he* didn't miss Patt.

"Just make a note of any calls you get and send them my way, all right?"

"Sure," Felix said, rubbing the back of his neck. "We just wanted to handle it before bothering you."

"Well, now I'm curious," I said, heading toward the back door. "Do you have a maintenance cart charged? It's too early for a hike to hole eleven."

Felix frowned. "You mean hole nine?"

I paused. "Wait. I thought the news said it was behind hole eleven."

Larry shrugged. "Tolbert's house backs up to eleven, but the light complaints came from the green at nine. Easy mistake — they're not far apart."

I frowned, picturing the course map in my head. He was right — the tee box for eleven sat close to the ninth green. I figured, since the news mentioned hole eleven and Mrs. Williams talked about spotlights on the green, they were talking about that green. Not the one beside it."

"Still a hike," I muttered, grabbing a cart key from the rack. Bruno hopped onto the back of the cart, tail sweeping the seat, while Felix sat by me.

"Let's go, partner," I said. "Seems like the morning just got more interesting."

The police spotlights came into view about halfway down the fairway, flickering faintly through the morning mist. The hole curved left, so the beams vanished again behind the trees before reappearing near the green — one of my least-favorite holes, with its tricky sand trap that had eaten more than one of my golf balls.

I parked the cart a respectful distance from the yellow crime tape surrounding Tolbert's house. Bruno jumped down first, nose to the ground, tail waving as he trotted toward the dew-damp grass.

"This is exactly how it looked," Felix said, climbing out behind me. "Last time I came out, the spotlights were right at the edge of the long grass. I swear it looked greener last week, though."

I followed him toward the green, studying the patchy rough. He was right — faint tire-like tracks curved through the dry leaves. "Don't worry about the turf," I told him. "The season's over. The grass will recover once spring hits."

Standing in the middle of the green, I looked toward the house. It had the same dark, modern siding I'd seen before, but now the deck looked oddly exposed — the trees, bare of leaves, no longer shielding it from view. Three houses across the street could see this spot clearly... unless something blocked the view.

As I stepped closer, the nearest spotlight flicked on automatically, flooding the house in harsh white glare. The sudden brightness startled Bruno, who barked once and trotted closer to me, ears perked.

"Boss, should we cover the sand trap?" Felix called. "Looks like something's getting into it."

I turned, frowning at the white dust speckled across the edge of the trap. "It should've been covered when the course closed," I said, walking up the small rise. "Did Patt order more sand before winter?"

Bruno padded after me, nose twitching, then started pawing at the edge of the trap. His deep whine made the hairs on my neck rise.

I walked over there and found the tarp tossed on the side and drag marks on the trap.

Like if something had gotten stuck on the it and pulled it open. "That's odd..."

When I glanced up to ask Felix again, my question froze on my tongue. From this angle, beneath Tolbert's deck, the boarded-up basement window was missing one of its planks. Shattered glass glinted faintly behind it.

"Felix," I said quietly, "did you notice that window before?"

He followed my gaze, eyes widening. "No, ma'am."

My pulse quickened. "Someone's been coming back here." I yanked my phone from my pocket and dialed 911.

Felix crouched beside me, whispering as if the intruder could still be lurking nearby. "How can you tell?"

I lowered my voice. "You said the spotlight was moved more than once, right?"

He nodded.

"That's the trick," I said. "Blinding the neighbors. If you shine a floodlight straight at their windows, no one can see what's happening out here. Whoever's been sneaking in used that light to cover their tracks."

Bruno gave a sharp bark, circling the trap again before sniffing toward the woods.

I thanked the dispatcher and hung up.

"Someone's used this spot as a path," I said. "The marks lead from the trap to the deck — and whatever's getting into that window isn't an animal."

Felix swallowed. "But how would they even reach this place? You can't drive out here without crossing half the course."

I clipped Bruno's leash, though he kept tugging toward the trees. "Not by cart," I murmured, scanning the slope. "There's another way in."

Felix frowned. "You think we'll catch them on the club's cameras?"

I shook my head. "Not if they knew where the cameras don't point."

Bruno barked again, pulling me toward the narrow tree line that separated the ninth green from the next fairway.

"Wait for the police," I told Felix, already stepping into the woods with Bruno leading the way. "I just need to check something."

Chapter 24

I t had been years since I'd walked this part of the golf course. After high school, I could count on one hand the number of times I'd played here — and I'd clearly forgotten more than I realized. All this time, I'd been picturing Tolbert's house on the opposite side of the hole, never once remembering the narrow path that cut through the trees.

As Bruno and I followed it, old memories came flooding back — sneaking out here after tournaments, daring each other to cross the creek barefoot — until my stomach dropped.

"Oh no," I whispered, quickening my pace. "Bruno, I think I just figured out how someone got in and out of the course."

The path opened into a small clearing, and sure enough, the stone footbridge came into view — the one that crossed beneath the fairway and followed the creek toward the city park. Golfers used it to stay on course, but if you went the opposite direction, it led straight to the public dock by the river.

Bruno barked once, trotting ahead. He didn't need my encouragement; his nose was already working overtime.

At the edge of the trees, the metallic storage rack came into view — the one our department used to store aquatic equipment for rentals. Norman's voice echoed in my head: *"We're missing a kayak."*

The rack looked ordinary from a distance, but as we got closer, the details stood out. One of the padlocks was badly scratched, the paint gouged where someone had forced it open. Bert would've spotted that right away, but Norman probably thought it was just wear and tear.

Bruno's tail stiffened as he sniffed the dirt around the rack, circling once before giving a low, uneasy growl. His hackles rose — and so did mine.

Then my phone buzzed violently in my pocket. I jumped and, embarrassingly, let out a yelp. "You almost gave me a heart attack!" I said, answering after checking the caller.

"I almost gave *you*—? Where in the world are you, Maggie?" Logan's voice carried that low, irritated edge I knew too well.

"I'm by the river. Why?"

A heavy sigh came through the line, followed by the muffled sound of him speaking to someone else. "She's by the river," he said, clearly reporting my location.

I frowned. "I'm not lost, Logan."

"When you make an emergency call, you're supposed to *stay put*," he said sharply. "Felix told me you walked into the woods. What were you thinking?"

I pressed my lips together. He wasn't wrong — but technically, I hadn't *left* the scene. I'd just expanded it.

"There's something you need to see," I said finally. "Do you know how to get to the river park?"

He didn't answer right away, but I could hear the engine start in the background.

"Of course I do," he said.

"I'll wait for you here. You'll understand when you see it."

Bruno gave a short bark as if agreeing that this discovery was worth the trouble — or maybe warning me that Logan wasn't going to be happy when he got here.

Logan stared at the scratched padlock for a long moment, saying nothing. He'd listened to every word I said without interrupting — which, honestly, was worse than if he'd cut me off. Silence from Detective Forest usually meant one thing: he was mad.

"Can you walk back to the course?" he finally asked.

"I can," I said carefully.

"How far is it?"

"Less than a mile."

His skeptical look made me sigh. "It's true. Driving around takes longer because of the river's bend. The golf course sits closer to the water than people realize. When they built it, the city kept it higher to avoid flooding — after a couple bad years of rain."

Logan fell into step behind me as we entered the narrow trail through the trees. Bruno trotted between us, his leash slack but his nose busy, tail flicking side to side.

"And you know all this because you're the R-Parks director?" Logan asked, his tone easing back to something more familiar — a mix of teasing and suspicion.

I glanced over my shoulder. "Of course not. I wrote a paper on Apple Creek's early river development back in college."

He laughed softly. "Of course you did. So that's how you knew about this secret path?"

"It's not secret," I said, rolling my eyes. "I learned about it in high school — during golf practice."

"Funny," he said. "We went to the same school, and I don't remember any path."

"Well, you never played golf, and Patt closed it during my senior year. He didn't like park-goers wandering onto the course. I doubt anyone ever did, but he put up signs anyway."

We reached the narrow creek crossing, and I stopped. Bruno sniffed the damp ground and gave a low huff. "This is where I think the suspect got away that night," I said quietly.

Logan's expression hardened immediately. He stepped off the trail, scanning both sides of the creek before crouching near the bank. Bruno followed, nose pressed to the earth. The detective's shoulders tensed.

"What's wrong?" I asked.

He stood again, hands on his hips. "What's wrong is that I'm not thrilled about organizing another search team out here — or realizing our suspect knows this place better than half the department." He gestured toward the water. "And if he made it to the river, that's miles of shoreline we'll have to cover."

That wasn't reassuring. Still, the question slipped out. "So you think he's from Apple Creek? Someone who knows every shortcut and back road?"

Logan nodded grimly. "Has to be."

We started back toward the fairway, Bruno padding just ahead, pausing every so often to sniff or glance over his shoulder. It took less than twenty minutes to reach the green again. I hated to admit it, but Logan was right — the suspect could have escaped easily that night, even with police flooding the area.

"You know what else bothers me?" Logan said as we neared the edge of the course. He waited until I met his eyes. "Why didn't you mention any of this before?"

I hesitated, brushing my hands together. "Because I thought Tolbert's house was by another hole. The news wasn't exactly clear about it — and Patt's off on vacation."

"What about Bert?" Logan asked. "Would he have known about this trail?"

Before I could answer, Tricia's voice called from the direction of the house. Logan looked at me once, then headed toward her.

The truth was, I didn't know. Maybe Bert knew the path existed. Maybe Tolbert did too. Maybe everyone who'd ever played a round here had known — and just never thought twice about it.

"Maggie!" Logan's voice broke through my thoughts. He was standing by the crime tape, waving me over. My stomach knotted at the memory of the last time he'd called me into a scene like that. It wasn't an ice rink this time, but the air had that same chill.

"I'll check if he knows anything else," he said to Tricia, then looked back at me. "You think you can drive me back to my car?"

That one surprised me, but I wasn't about to argue.

Chapter 25

L arry greeted us with steaming mugs of coffee and the delicious smell of cinnamon buds — a smell that should've come with an award. Sadly, I didn't get to eat any. Logan had to get back to the station, and I probably should've gone to the office.

"I just want it on record," I said as we walked out, "that someone owes me a proper breakfast for this sacrifice."

"Noted," Logan said, clearly distracted by the phone buzzing in his hand.

Bruno jumped into the back seat, curling up like a well-trained pro. I walked around to the driver's side, but before I could open the door, Logan was there, holding it for me — even while answering his call.

"Let me put you on speaker," he said as he slid into the passenger seat. "Maggie's here."

"Oh, hi Maggie!" Arthur's voice filled the car. I hadn't expected that. Then again, I hadn't expected Logan to announce I was there either.

"Hi Arthur," I said, smiling faintly.

Logan didn't waste time with small talk. "So let me get this straight — the remains are about a century old, but not who we thought they belonged to?"

There was a burst of shuffling and papers crackling on the other end.

"Correct," Arthur said. "We found a button found among the remains was manufactured mainly in France around that era, which initially made us think it belonged to Thomas Deaport. We couldn't extract DNA — not surprising, given the age — but osteological analysis confirmed the skeleton was male. And here's where it gets interesting."

I felt Bruno's head nudge between the seats, as if he could sense this was one of *those* conversations.

Arthur continued, voice buzzing through the speaker. "I checked with the county clerk. Their ledgers show Thomas Deaport married a woman named Ruth Mary Dorothy..." He paused, then added a last name I didn't catch. "Thomas was twenty-eight."

"That's considered old?" I frowned. "What does that make me?"

Arthur chuckled. "Different times, Maggie. Ruth was about nineteen — as best as I can tell without her birth record."

"That explains why no one knew if she had a sister," Logan said.

"Exactly," Arthur replied. "But here's the twist. Based on the fusion of the skull sutures, pelvis, and long bone growth plates, the remains belong to someone between eighteen and twenty."

I instinctively eased the car to a stop. "So it *can't* be Thomas."

"Exactly!" Arthur said, clearly enjoying the revelation. "And it gets darker. This young man's remains show defensive wounds — fractured ribs, wrist trauma — and a severe skull fracture at the back of the head. Likely struck hard from behind after a fight."

I shivered, my hand instinctively reaching toward Bruno's fur. He gave a low, comforting rumble, as if he'd sensed the chill running down my spine.

Arthur hesitated before adding, "Sorry,

Maggie. I know that's gruesome, but this was definitely murder."

Logan's jaw tightened. "Thanks, Arthur. I'll see you at the station soon."

"Bye, Arthur," I said.

I pulled up next to Logan's car, my head spinning with new info. "Hey, Logan what if..."

"What is it?" Logan asked.

I chewed on my lip. "Just thinking. If we take Thelma, Rose, and Walter at their word, Thomas was... not exactly a saint, right?"

"According to them," Logan said carefully.

"So maybe Thomas killed George — the cousin who claimed the farm. Ruth finds out and tells Franklyn, who uses it to force Thomas to 'leave for Europe' while he stays behind with Ruth."

Logan stared at me for a long moment, unreadable as ever. Then, without a word, he opened his door, stepped out, and leaned against it, arms crossed.

"Do *not* go trying to test that theory on your own, Maggie."

I raised my hands in mock surrender. "What, am I supposed to interrogate the body?"

"Not the body. Not the goats.

Not *anyone.*" His tone softened, though. "Promise me."

I smiled, knowing he wasn't half as amused as I was pretending to be. "Sure. I promise not to investigate this imaginary century-old conspiracy without you."

He still didn't look convinced, so he glanced at Bruno. "You heard her, partner. Keep her out of trouble."

Bruno perked up, tail thumping against the seat.

"Traitor," I told him, scratching his ear.

Logan chuckled, stepping back. "See you soon, Maggie."

As he headed for his car, Bruno let out one last soft *woof,* like he was sealing the deal — a canine pinky promise that I'd probably break before the week was out.

Before I even made it to my office, I spotted Sophie and Miss Tony huddled near Linda's desk. Sophie's eyes were red and puffy, and both women were talking over each other in the kind of heated whisper that could be heard across the hallway.

"That's ridiculous!" Linda said, throwing her hands up.

"Not ridiculous," Miss Tony countered, "strategic. We need to lure him out. Set a trap."

There was no way to sneak past unnoticed —and honestly, I wanted to know what had reduced Sophie to tears. I touched her shoulder, and Bruno immediately pressed his head under her hand, tail swishing gently as if to say *you're safe now.*

"What happened?" I asked softly.

Sophie opened her mouth but couldn't get the words out. Miss Tony, of course, took command.

"Well, Margaret," she said with a grim sigh, "we heard that your lawyer friend, Mr. Klauer, was released on bail. Poor Sophie here tried to find out about Bert—and he didn't make bail."

A guilty pang hit me. I kind of figured this out after what Henry said at my mom's house. Still I asked.

"Why not?"

Linda shook her head, tapping a folder on her desk. "According to the judge, Bert's considered a bigger flight risk than Henry. Probably because Henry's staying at Logan's house, practically under supervision. House arrest, really. But Miss Tony thinks there's another reason."

Miss Tony straightened proudly, chin lifted. "Not a *theory*, Margaret. A *fact*. I talked to the judge, and he spilled the beans."

I didn't even want to know how she managed that. I was no longer surprised by anything Miss Tony could charm—or terrify—out of someone.

"The police believe this killer has to be from Apple Creek," she went on. "And since Bert was an old friend of the singer, poor Billy Tolbert, they're afraid he'll bolt before the real suspect is caught."

"But Bert would never hurt anyone!" Sophie cried, voice cracking. "He's a victim in all of this! Why haven't you helped him?"

Her words hit hard. She clapped a trembling hand over her mouth. "I'm sorry—I didn't mean that. I'm just—he's still in a cell, and they might send him to prison soon. I can't—"

I wrapped an arm around her. Bruno leaned against her legs, solid and warm. "Sophie, we'll figure this out. Bert wasn't the only friend Tolbert had."

"Exactly!" Miss Tony said. "Do you still have those yearbooks, Margaret?"

We moved into my office, and Miss Tony wasted no time spreading the heavy books across my desk. She flipped pages like a professional historian until she stopped on one of Bert's senior-year photos.

"This is our guy," she declared, tapping the picture.

I leaned closer. The photo showed Bert with an electric guitar slung over his shoulder, Billy Tolbert grinning beside him. On the far end stood a boy with dark hair, oversized sunglasses, and his arms crossed.

"Who's that?" I asked.

Linda squinted. "It says 'Terry F. Johnson.'"

Sophie gasped. "I've heard that name! He used to be Billy's manager. He was accused of fraud years ago."

Miss Tony slapped the page triumphantly. "There! My point exactly. Bad apple from the start. He's the one who killed Billy. I'd bet my roses on it."

"But the police haven't found him," Sophie said. "He's been missing for years! They said he stole almost half a million dollars. Maybe more."

Miss Tony crossed her arms. "Then we find

him first. He's the reason all this started—and I know how to smoke him out."

"Oh no," Linda muttered. "Here it comes."

Miss Tony's eyes gleamed. "We send the goats back to the barn."

"The goats?" I repeated, half-laughing. "Miss Tony, we don't even know the motive yet —or if this murder is connected to the farm."

"Maggie," she said, leaning across my desk as if sharing state secrets, "trust me. This kind of man—clever, cocky, thinks he's playing games—he'll circle back to the scene. You'll see. My husband's FBI cases were *full* of these types. Those jars, the pearls, the creepy dolls— it's all a distraction. Either he's hiding something in that barn or working with those women. And tell me—who doesn't lose their mind over losing that kind of fortune?"

She didn't wait for our answer. "So we bait him. He'll come for the goats, and we'll be ready."

"Who's coming for what goats?" a voice asked from the doorway.

We all jumped at once—Sophie gasped, Linda squeaked, Miss Tony clutched her necklace, and Bruno barked sharply, hackles raised before recognizing the voice.

Logan stood in the doorway, arms crossed, the perfect image of an amused but very tired detective.

Chapter 26

Logan didn't look the least bit amused when he stepped fully into the room. His expression was the same one I'd seen on Ben during council meetings—patient, but one breath away from an explosion.

"So," he said, scanning each of us, "whose trap are we talking about?"

Miss Tony didn't flinch. Crossing her arms, she stood tall and declared, "You have the wrong man, Detective." She put heavy emphasis on *Detective,* as if it were an accusation. "Poor Bert is innocent. So is your friend Henry. This is your guy."

She tapped the photo on my desk.

"His name's Terry Johnson," Sophie added quickly, her voice still shaky. "He was Billy Tolbert's manager. He committed fraud—millions —and he's from Apple Creek."

Logan's jaw tightened, but he didn't speak. Linda took that as her cue to jump in. "You have to arrest him. It's obvious! He killed Billy for the money, and since he knows the city, he's been hiding right under your noses."

Miss Tony nodded in solemn agreement. "That's why we need to lure him out. He's been two steps ahead of the police this entire time."

Logan exhaled sharply and stepped forward, his tone rising just enough to silence the room. "Of *course* we know this." His hand cut through the air toward the yearbook. "And yes, Johnson is a person of interest—along with others I'm not going to discuss with any of you."

Miss Tony opened her mouth again. "So if we set a—"

"You won't set anything," Logan snapped, and this time his voice carried the full weight of command. "That's not a suggestion, Miss Tony. That's an order."

Bruno gave a soft rumble beside me, as if agreeing.

Logan continued, lower but more dangerous. "You're talking about a multi-murderer who knows this city better than most officers on my team. He's armed, he's unpredictable, and if you get in his way, he will kill you."

The room fell into heavy silence. Even Miss Tony hesitated, her fingers tightening on the yearbook's spine.

Linda swallowed. "We—we understand," she murmured.

Logan turned a measured look toward Miss Tony. "Do I make myself clear?"

She rolled her eyes just enough to keep her pride intact. "Yes, Detective Forest," she said, clipped but audible.

He studied her for a moment, then sighed and stepped aside. "Good. Now, if you'll all excuse me, I need a word with Maggie."

Nobody moved. Linda shuffled awkwardly, Sophie stood frozen, and for a horrifying second, I thought Miss Tony was about to sit down again.

"I mean in private," Logan clarified, louder this time, holding the door open pointedly.

Linda mumbled an apology and hurried out. Sophie followed without looking up, wiping her eyes as she passed Bruno, who sniffed her hand sympathetically.

Miss Tony lingered, her mischievous smile already returning. "Oh, and Detective—tell

Arthur his father and I are going to dinner tonight, so he should stay home."

Logan blinked, visibly torn between disbelief and respect. "Of course, Miss Tony."

She nodded, satisfied, and swept out of the room with her stack of yearbooks.

The door clicked shut, leaving only Bruno's quiet tail thump and the faint hum of Logan's frustration filling my office.

The moment Logan closed the door behind him, I realized something was wrong. He checked both windows, then the hallway, before finally turning back to me. His expression was drawn tight—serious enough that my heart dropped.

"Is everything all right?" I asked, bracing for the kind of news that makes your stomach twist.

He pushed a hand through his hair and exhaled. "Tricia and I went to talk with Mr. Gray."

It took me a second to catch up—Walter Gray, the city historian. I hadn't expected him to come up again so soon.

Logan hesitated before continuing. "Someone broke into the senior living facility last night. No security footage, no witnesses in the parking lot, but..." He looked down, his voice dropping. "Mr. Gray is dead."

My hand flew to my mouth. "What—how? Why?"

He shook his head. "We don't know yet. It wasn't a robbery. Tolbert's house was broken into again too—same night. The only rooms disturbed were his office and the vault in his bedroom. Whoever did it knew exactly where to look. But nothing obvious was taken. No money, no valuables—just papers, maybe. We wanted to ask Mr. Gray more about the farm, and now..." He trailed off.

I sank back in my chair. "Clearly he *did* know something."

Logan sat down across from me. His face looked as worn as his voice sounded. Bruno padded over from his spot by the door and rested his head on Logan's knee. Logan scratched behind his ear absently as he spoke.

"We think the killer may have taken old documents—property records, family ledgers. The bank confirmed Walter had a safe deposit box, but we can't access it without a warrant or his lawyer."

I folded my arms, trying to steady my thoughts. "Did you check who visited him recently?"

He nodded. "Yeah. He had plenty of company—council members, the city attorney, some of the residents. But..." He leaned closer, lowering his tone. "Don't tell Miss Tony—or anyone—but it looks like Johnson might be more tangled up in this than we thought. He was Walter's nephew."

I stared at him. "Walter's *nephew*? The same Terry Johnson who stole millions?"

Logan gave a grim nod. "We don't know if Walter knew about the fraud, but we'll find out once we can access his accounts. The timing's too close, Maggie. And there's more—Walter's full name was *Walter Franklyn Gray.*"

The realization hit like ice water. "Franklyn? As in Thomas Deaport's brother?"

"Exactly. Which means Walter knew about the barn legend because it wasn't a legend for him—it was family history. He just didn't tell us the whole truth."

I swallowed hard. "And now he's dead."

Logan rubbed his hands over his face. "Yeah. Being murdered's a strong indication someone's hiding something." He paused, exhaled, then added, "And that's not all."

The seconds between his words stretched like forever.

"I got a call from the city waterfront guard," he said finally. "They found your missing kayak."

Something in me—some tight, anxious part—loosened. "You believed me."

He frowned. "Of course I believe you, Maggie. I might question *how* you end up in the middle of these things, but I never doubt you."

I smiled, just a little. "That's nice to hear."

His next words cut through the warmth. "The kayak wasn't on the riverbank. It was lodged inside the water-treatment filter system. Someone must've dumped it there. It's in pieces, but the city logo's still visible."

My relief vanished. "So it wasn't lost by accident."

"No," he said quietly. "It wasn't."

He stood, clearly preparing to go. "I have to head into the city. The evidence is being processed there, and Tricia wants to coordinate with their forensic unit."

"How long will you be gone?" I asked, hating how small my voice sounded.

"Just as long as necessary," he said. "I'll be back late tonight, or early tomorrow." He reached for the door, then hesitated. Maggie, are you and Darcy interested in going somewhere this weekend? I know you have the festival preparations, but... I don't know. This case it's different. Maybe a change of scenery with fresh air would be nice?"

"I hear the train ride up to Maple Hollow it's pretty over the season."

He smiled and tapped the frame of the door. "Sounds like a great plan."

As he turned to leave, I heard my own voice slip out before I could stop it. "Are you taking Bruno?"

He looked down at his partner, who sat obediently by his boot, eyes bright and loyal. Logan crouched and scratched under his chin. "Not this time, buddy." He whispered something I couldn't hear, then stood. "He's staying with you."

"Will you let me know when you're on your way back?"

He smiled—warm, but weary. "Promise."

Then he paused in the doorway, glancing back at us. "Take care of our girls, Bruno."

Bruno gave a low, steady *woof.*

I wasn't sure whether it comforted me or made the office feel even emptier.

Chapter 27

My phone buzzed against the nightstand, dragging me out of a deep sleep. The room was still dark, and for a second I couldn't tell if it was midnight or morning.

"Norman?" My voice came out rough. "What happened? Isn't like midnight?"

"Sadly, it's almost five," he said, sounding just as tired. "And we've got a problem."

I rubbed my eyes, still half-asleep. "What kind of problem?"

There was a pause—too long—and then Norman sighed. "Someone, and by someone I mean *Miss Tony,* decided to release the goats at the farm."

"The *what?*"

That woke me up faster than any cup of

coffee ever could. I sat straight up, heart racing. "You're joking."

"I wish," Norman said, the sound of rustling papers and shuffling feet in the background. "Harold Whitestone called me. You know—the janitor from the Community Center?"

"Harold? How would *he* even know?" I was already halfway to my closet, trying to put on jeans and think at the same time.

"Remember we're moving the vendor supplies from the Community Center to the farm this morning? He said when he got there, the goats were already roaming around like they owned the place."

"Oh no," I groaned, as I remembered Miss Tony's trap idea.

"I was going to handle it myself," Norman said, "but with the barn closed, there's nowhere to put them—and I don't have time to chase goats before sunrise."

"I'm on my way," I said, grabbing my keys. "Try to gather them near the fence if you can, but don't spook them. I'll figure out where to keep them until we open the farm for the festival."

Bruno was already waiting by the door, tail thumping against the wall. He gave me a big yawn and a look that clearly said *finally, something interesting.*

"Well," I muttered, pulling on my jacket, "at least one of us is thrilled to work before dawn."

He trotted beside me as I locked up and hurried to the car.

The roads were empty except for the fog that lingered like a blanket over the fields. I gripped the steering wheel tighter as the farm's outline came into view.

"Bruno," I said, glancing at him through the rearview mirror, "we might have to test your herding skills today."

He gave a short, confident *woof*, tail wagging.

"Good," I said. "Because if Miss Tony's goats are wandering loose at five in the morning, I'm starting to think she's more dangerous than the actual suspect."

The first light of dawn spread over the farm in soft pink tones when I pulled into the parking lot a little after five. The scene was peaceful, almost too peaceful.

Rose's confession replayed in my mind—how she'd said it was too dark to see anything that morning. But that didn't make sense. If she'd been here a week earlier, it would've been *darker* then. And daylight savings hadn't changed yet.

"This is odd, Bruno," I muttered.

He gave a low whine from the passenger seat, ears pricked.

As I turned toward Norman's truck, a goat darted across the entrance, its shadow flickering in the early light. I barely had time to register it when my phone rang. Logan's name flashed on the screen, and despite the chaos, I smiled.

"Early morning, Detective?"

He cleared his throat. "I know, sorry. Just keeping my promise. I'm on my way back—took longer than expected, and probably a waste of time."

"That's not good," I said, turning off the ignition. "Maybe we could meet for an early breakfast before you get some sleep?"

He gave a soft laugh. "Breakfast? Isn't it about three hours early for you?"

"Maybe just one and a half," I teased, opening the door. "And by the way, I'm already working."

I stepped onto the gravel. "Bruno, I'll go around and open your door."

The air was cool and smelled faintly of hay and damp earth. But something about the stillness felt... wrong.

Then everything happened too fast.

A flash of movement—Norman lying on the ground beside his truck. A shadow shifting toward me. My car door slamming shut behind.

"Breakfast sounds great, Maggie," Logan said through the phone—but his voice sounded miles away as my stomach dropped.

The man's voice that followed was much closer. Calm. Cold. "Finish your conversation, Margaret. But don't try anything silly."

Francis Terrance stood inches away, pointing a gun at my face.

I forced a steady breath and lifted the phone again. "Linda," I said, praying he hadn't heard Logan's name. "Friday's booked on my agenda, and I don't think there are any night trains to the city. We'll talk later, all right?"

"Maggie?" Logan's tone sharpened, instantly suspicious. "Where are you?"

I hung up and locked the screen before the man could see the name.

"We won't need this." Francis snatched the

phone and tossed it aside. "Or him." He pointed inside the car, where Bruno's bark tore through the quiet morning, deep and furious.

"I'll admit, I was worried I'd have to shoot him. I don't like animal violence."

Francis's mouth curved into something like a smirk. "I need to get into the barn, and I hear *you* have the key."

He motioned with the gun for me to move.

"Did you kill Norman?" I asked as I stepped forward.

He pressed the barrel lightly against my back. "I don't know," he said flatly. "And I don't care. Just keep walking."

I turned toward the farmhouse, and he grabbed my arm, pulling me back hard.

"Where do you think you're going?"

"To get the keys," I snapped, jerking my arm free. "They're in the farmhouse. Why would I keep barn keys in my pocket? I don't even have my mom's house keys with me."

He studied me for a moment, then gestured toward the porch. "Go."

Anger replaced the fear crawling up my spine. I *should* have realized sooner. The rental car parked at City Hall for days, the kayak found down in the city—I should have checked the train's schedule. All the clues had been there.

"There aren't nighttime trains to the city, right?"

He smirked but remained quiet.

"Is Maple Hollow even changing names?" I asked when we reached the door.

He chuckled softly. "Oh yes. I wouldn't lie about my job, Margaret. I took Park management very seriously."

I frowned as I unlocked the door. "So the festival was your excuse to get close to the farm? To steal a family treasure?"

His jaw tightened, eyes hard. He lifted the gun slightly, and I caught the glint of metal in the morning light. "This place belongs to *my side of the family. Those Jacobson women took advantage of an old family tradition and tried to outsmart my uncle. Ironically, their ridiculous idea to scare people off here after my uncle added the goats on the barn, and Bill's foolishness is what made me realized what was happening.*"

My hands trembled as I opened the desk drawer. "You mean Thelma and Rose were working with Tolbert?"

Francis leaned over the desk, close enough for me to smell the sharp tang of gun oil. "Bill betrayed me. First, he tried to buy the farm, but he was too late. Those Jacobson losers already sold it. Then, he pretended to be me and tried to convince my uncle to claim the ownership of the farm. To steal my money. Always the fool."

The truth hit me like a slap. "Miss Tony was right," I whispered. "You're Terry F. Johnson. *F* as in Franklyn. Franklyn close to Francis. You committed the fraud with Billy. All those concerts and events—you used the cash flow to hide your cut. The bags of small bills in the barn... they're yours."

He smiled then, a proud, awful smile. "You *are* clever. I knew I liked you."

"So Tolbert tried to betray you—get the farm to keep the money—but Thelma sold it to the city to protect her family legacy?"

Francis shook his head. "You give her too much credit. None of them cared about the legacy. They just wanted the money."

He motioned toward the door again. "Now hurry up. I'm not a monster, Margaret. I don't want to leave a child without a mother."

The words froze me. My fingers brushed the cold metal keys in the drawer. I lifted them slowly and held them out.

"Shall we?" he said, smirking as he motioned for me to lead the way.

My hands were shaking so much I could barely fit the key into the padlock. Francis loomed behind me, silent but close enough that I could feel his breath on my neck.

The key finally clicked, and the chain clattered to the ground.

"You know what's funny?" he said, shoving me against the wall as he kicked one of the barn doors open. "That little prank Rose pulled with the jars and the creepy doll." He chuckled, stepping inside. "That's what tipped me off. I wouldn't have suspected Bill's concert if I hadn't heard that ridiculous story in the paper."

He turned the gun toward me. "Walk."

I stepped forward, the air inside the barn thick with hay dust and old secrets. Dim light filtered through the high windows. Something moved in the rafters above, faint and muffled.

"Add the goats..." I muttered under my breath.

He jabbed the gun into my back. "What?"

"You convinced your uncle to add the goats. Once the city took ownership, the best way to hide your money was to keep the stalls occupied. But Thelma didn't want them..."

He smirked, watching me.

"Your side of the family?" I asked. "You're not a Deaport like Thelma and Rose—you're a descendant of George. The one Thomas killed."

He shoved me into the same stall where we'd found the body. The crime tape fluttered as I ducked under it.

"Smart. Very smart," he sneered. "My uncle was obsessed with that nonsense. I never cared about it, though. I used the legend to hide my own treasure here, that used to be all. Who owns this dump wouldn't matter to me. But then, Billy tried to sneak around it, and I learned some very interesting things about the barn. Now, since the police took my money, I'm going to take what it's rightfully mine— George's inheritance."

He ran a hand along the edge of the stall, tapping the wood as if searching for something.

"Inheritance..." I whispered. "George brought something back from Europe. Thomas tried to steal it, and when the fight broke out—"

Francis snapped, pressing the barrel against

my ribs. "Where is it? Did the police find the key?"

"A key? What—I don't know!" My voice cracked, but my confusion must've sounded real, because he pulled the gun away and turned back to the boards.

"My uncle must've hidden it here," he muttered to himself. "I searched his place on Saturday before I kill—Tolbert ruined everything."

A shadow crossed the small window above us. I looked up—and nearly screamed. One of the goats stood in the loft, staring down, its eyes glinting red in the half-light.

Francis noticed my reaction and followed my gaze. "Jumping at goats now, Margaret?" he said dryly, crouching. His hand brushed something in the hay. "Ah. There you are." He pried a loose plank up and shoved his hand beneath the floorboards.

"You know your uncle's dead," I said.

That made him freeze.

"He was murdered last night," I added quietly.

He turned slowly, his face pale. "No. He's in the senior living. They would've contact—" He stopped, realization sinking in. "Tolbert!

He changed my contact information. That lying—"

Sirens wailed in the distance, growing closer.

Francis cursed and yanked me to my feet. "What did you do?"

Before I could answer, a voice thundered from behind the open barn door.

"Drop it, Francis!"

Thelma Jacobson stood there, braced and wild-eyed, holding a shotgun that looked far too heavy for her. Her hands trembled, but her voice didn't.

"You won't take my fortune," she loaded a round. "I grew up thinking how ridiculous all this Deaport's stories were. Too much drama and nothing worth it. Then, your friend shows up, demanding the farm as his own and swearing he will put me in jail if I had taken his fortune. George's treasure! That's my treasure!"

Francis actually laughed—a sharp, bitter sound. "Poor Thelma! You never thought in searching you own property for decades?" he pushed me back, and I lost my balance right before hitting the stall's wall with the back of my head.

My vision blurred, but I saw him lifting his gun. "What a loser!"

I heard Thelma scream right before a loud shot that muffled my hearing.

A second blast echoed through the barn, and I got a sight of how the recoil threw her backward into the haystack.

The shotgun clattered to the floor, and before I could react, Francis limped towards her, gun in hand.

"You killed my uncle—You are so dead!"

A blur of brown fur tore through the barn. Bruno.

He hit Francis with the force of a storm, teeth sinking into his arm before the gun could rise again. The man screamed, twisting and falling hard onto the boards.

"Put the gun down!" someone shouted behind me.

Red and blue lights flickered through the open doors as more voices filled the barn. Bruno held fast, growling low and fierce.

I tried to stand up, but a pair of hands gently held me back.

"Maggie—don't move," Logan said somehow kneeling in front of me.

"I'm fine," I managed, though my words

slurred slightly and the world around me seemed to be spinning.

"Sure you are," he said, pulling my hand down before I touched the back of my head. "Stay still." He turned to the others. "Get a medic in here—now!"

Bruno finally released Francis's arm when Logan called him back, his chest heaving, fur matted with hay and sweat. He trotted straight to me, tail low, eyes searching.

"It's okay," I whispered, petting his head with a trembling hand. "Good boy."

Logan petted him too. "Really good boy," he exclaimed. "You found her." His voice lowed as he leaned closer to my ear. "But why are the goats here?"

Chapter 28

I sat in the farmhouse's fake kitchen, holding an ice pack to the back of my head and trying to keep a wool blanket from the gift shop wrapped around my shoulders. Everything suddenly felt cold.

Bruno hadn't left my side since he'd leapt into the barn and attacked Francis. I was grateful for him—but I still felt awful for leaving him locked in the car.

The last thing I'd heard was that Norman was on his way to the hospital, but he was going to be fine. He'd been hit in the head with the back of a gun. Someone had found two of the goats wandering near the garden, and the third had finally decided to join its siblings on the ground.

"Tricia said Miss Tony's fine," Ben was

telling an officer by the door. "And we found the truck that Francis used to steal the goats from her backyard. I have no idea what he was thinking."

I had a pretty good idea. Poor Miss Tony. Norman and I had blindly blamed her for the goats being here, but that didn't make sense. She loved those four. She'd told me as much before—when she made me promise not to bring them back until the barn was restored and safe.

Instead, it had been Francis who wanted the barn opened at that early hour. He was the one who called and complained about the goats, forcing Norman first—and then me—to come to the farm. Why hadn't he just broken the padlock, the way he did with the one on the kayaks? A cold shiver ran down my spine, and I shook my head. I didn't want to think about what Francis might have done to get away.

"I'll take Maggie to the hospital," I heard Logan say. That wasn't going to happen.

"I'm fine," I said, standing.

Logan rushed over and tried to get me to sit back down, but I shook my head.

"I'm not going to any hospital."

He opened his mouth to argue, but I cut

him off. "I'm not scaring Darcy or my mom. I just bumped my head. He didn't hurt me."

Logan looked to Ben, who didn't seem pleased. But I wasn't either. I hadn't planned any of this, and he had no right to be mad—not this time. I'd kept my promise. I was doing my job.

"Maggie," Logan said carefully, "let me just take you so they can make sure you don't have a concussion—"

I grabbed his arm and stared at him. "Francis didn't kill Walter."

Logan nodded. "We know."

Ben started to protest, but Logan stopped him. "She has a right to know, Chief."

Ben groaned, threw up his hands, and walked deeper into the house.

"Thelma was pretty loud when she shot Francis," Logan continued. "After that, we sent a patrol to check her house. Tricia found Rose trying to run." He exhaled. "Rose confessed. Tolbert had met her months ago and paid her to scare her aunt out of the farm. He didn't realize the city already owned it, and when he found out, he threatened her."

I covered my mouth and shook my head. "I guess Thelma didn't want to help her?"

Logan nodded. "After the prank, Thelma

got furious and forced Rose to help her 'fix' their family legacy. Thelma already knew about the bags of money and had been taking from them. When we seized it all, she panicked and decided to chase the so-called family treasure. Rose saw Thelma strike Walter with his cane after he told her the treasure belonged to his side of the family—to him and his nephew, not them.'"

I pulled the blanket tighter around my shoulders. "So Thelma went back to the barn to look again—but found Francis and me instead?"

Logan nodded. "Francis wanted to make sure we'd only found the money in the wall. Unfortunately for him, he was about to learn we'd uncovered the big stash underneath the barn—another twenty bags."

"Underneath the barn?" I said. "That's—no. He was looking for the *family treasure*, Logan. He found a key in the stall."

Logan frowned. "And you think that key opens some kind of treasure from the nineteenth century?"

"Yes. Something George Deaport brought back from Europe."

Ben crossed his arms. "Wait a second. Why

didn't anyone take all the bags earlier, when we didn't know about them?"

I shrugged and raised an eyebrow. "Because it's difficult to hide that much money. Francis clearly took his time using it—that's how he moved around without being noticed by city cameras. He'd done it for years. And Thelma didn't have the criminal sense to launder anything."

Ben narrowed his eyes. "I'm not sure I like how fast you figure these things out, young lady."

"Well, where's the rest of George's treasure then?" Logan asked.

I shrugged—then remembered what Walter had said about the Deaports' legacy. "Dorothy got the farm," I murmured. "George got the investments but supposedly lost them gambling. But he didn't. He came back from Europe. He couldn't have gone far..."

I looked up at them and smiled. "The goats. It's always been about the goats."

I didn't really need help walking, but I wasn't about to push Logan away from holding my arm as we made our way to the barn. He lifted the crime tape for me and Ben, then followed us inside. Bruno, of course, stayed right by my side.

The workbench stood against the far wall near the stalls. It wasn't as clean as the last time Logan and I were here, but someone had clearly been searching around it. I crouched down and gave a closer look at the engravings on the drawer. With a flashlight it was easy to recognize the little jumping goats on them. I slid it open, it was empty—so I pulled the entire drawer out and kneeled to look underneath.

Now Francis's key, the one he'd found in the stall, made total sense.

On the side of the workbench's leg, near the far end just below the top, was a tiny keyhole. If I hadn't been for the insistence on Ruth's love for her goats, I would have never found it.

"If you have the key," I said, "I'm sure you can find it."

Logan held up a clear plastic evidence bag containing the key, and handed me a pair of latex gloves. "You found it. You get the honors."

I grinned and tugged the gloves on as fast as

I could. Finding a treasure was something I'd only dreamed about when I was little—playing pirate with Sandie in our backyard—or more recently, with Darcy during her "detective" games.

The key slid in perfectly. It took a little wiggling, but then I heard a soft click, and the side panel of the workbench popped open. A puff of fine white dust floated out, and when I waved it away, I saw several small velvet bags tucked neatly inside.

I picked one up, surprised at the weight that nearly pulled my hand down. When I loosened the drawstring, at least twenty gold coins spilled out, clinking as they scattered across the dusty barn floor.

"And I'm guessing that's not the only bag?" Logan asked, his smile every bit as boyish as mine felt.

I shook my head and crawled out from under the workbench. "I suppose it's all evidence now?"

Ben was smiling too, though he still managed a fatherly tone. "You can't keep the treasure, Maggie. But I'm sure your mom will be disappointed about it."

I smiled and sat on a nearby stool, Bruno pressing against my leg while Logan carefully lifted the remaining bags out from under the workbench. Watching him tag and count each one, I felt the tension that had been twisting inside me for days finally ease.

The case was over.

The treasure was real.

And, as the weight of everything settled, I realized all I wanted now was to go home, curl up with Darcy—and maybe take a nap in the sun like Bruno.

Epilogue

T he concert at the festival was loud, cheerful, and packed. After all the news about the hidden treasure and the "goats' mystery," we had more visitors than ever. Good for the city, great for the vendors. The Mayor of the newly renamed *Ever Hollow* had even apologized to me personally for the behavior of his former employee—and, of course, he wanted to set dates for next year's festival, complete with train rides as part of the celebration.

I decided to let our own Mayor and the council figure that one out.

Still, I'd learned a few surprising things about my city. For example, Bert was actually a talented electric guitar player who hadn't joined Billy Tolbert's band because his parents insisted he go to college. And as my lovely sister reminded me, Henry used to sing and play bass back in high school—for fun.

As a thank-you for my help, the two of them reunited to perform at the Fall Festival concert. They weren't famous, but the crowd loved them. Familiar songs, local faces—it was the perfect ending to a chaotic few weeks.

"Mommy!" Darcy shouted as she sprinted from the pumpkin-decorating stand, chased by Toby and my mom. "Can we get some apple stuff?"

I knelt down to hear her better. "Apple stuff?"

She waved her little hands dramatically, describing a very detailed bowl of apple crisp with ice cream—complete with the claim that it was "super healthy."

"It's made with apples, Mom. And milk. Ice cream is just frozen milk."

I laughed but gave in. Who was I to argue with that logic? Although, I did make a mental note to take her to Mrs. O'Leary's shop soon so she could learn exactly how ice cream was *really* made.

"I guess we got something good out of all

the mayhem," Linda called, approaching with Miss Tony at her side.

Linda pointed toward the stage, where I spotted Sophie right in the front row. For such a shy girl, she was practically glowing—especially with Bert on stage, grinning down at her like he was playing just for her.

"That's good," I said with a smile. "Although I'm not sure our city lawyer would approve."

Linda waved her hand dismissively. "Oh, Margaret, let her have her moment."

"Margaret," Miss Tony said, grabbing my hand and leaning in so I could hear her over the music. "I promise you—I had *nothing* to do with the goats at the farm. I know I mentioned the idea in your office, but I swear, I didn't do it. How could I?"

If anyone could've arranged a secret goat relocation, it was Miss Tony—but we knew the truth. Francis had broken into her backyard and moved the goats himself to confuse everyone. He confessed it was a message to Thelma: it was *his* farm, and he was in charge of it.

"I know, Miss Tony," I said. "I'm sorry we couldn't send them back afterward. City rules can be... complicated."

She patted my arm with approval. "Well, if you need a home for them, you know where to find me."

Arthur appeared then, half dancing, half singing along to the music.

"Oh, Arthur," Miss Tony exclaimed. "How are you ever going to get married with *those* moves?"

Arthur rolled his eyes but didn't reply—he knew better than to argue with her. Instead, he turned to me.

"Logan was looking for you," he said, pointing toward the vendor section at the back. "I think he needs rescuing—from Mrs. Williams, or something like that."

I laughed, apologized to Linda and Miss Tony, and made my way through the crowd toward the vendors. The music, the laughter, and the crisp fall air filled the night. Somewhere ahead, I could already picture Logan trying to charm his way out of Mrs. Williams's flower lectures—and I knew exactly who would have to save him.

Bruno trotted beside me, tail wagging like he knew the way.

The music wasn't as loud back there, and the mix of spices and apple cider made the night feel warmer than it was. I slowed down, searching for the flower stand, but suddenly Bruno tugged me off to the side.

"Slow down, Bruno," I said—then stopped when I saw Logan walking toward us.

"There you are," he said, and before I could reply, he pulled his arm from behind his back, revealing a bouquet of flowers. "They're not as pretty as you are, but I thought you might like these."

My gaze fell to the yellow and white blooms he handed me.

"You see," he continued, stepping closer, "Mrs. Williams wasn't thrilled when I asked for these. She said I should be buying red roses or something more romantic. But... well, I know what you call Darcy sometimes."

The words echoed in my mind as I looked down at the sunflowers—realizing just how closely he'd been paying attention to us. To *me*.

When I looked up, he was right in front of me, looking down with that soft, familiar smile.

"Love them," I whispered.

His smile deepened. He lifted his hands,

brushed a strand of hair behind my ear, and pulled me closer. One second I was looking at him, and the next, my eyes were closed as I kissed him back.

It wasn't a long kiss, but before I could even process it, a small voice broke through the music.

"Mommy! Mommy! He did it!"

I pulled back just as my knees decided to stop working—thankfully, Logan's arm was there to catch me.

"Sunflower," I said, turning toward her, "who did what? Toby?"

Darcy skidded to a stop in front of us, bouncing with excitement. "Ben! Ben did it, Mommy! He asked Grandma!"

I turned, and sure enough, Sandie was nodding toward me, her smile wide as she motioned for us to come over.

"Did Grandma say yes?"

Darcy frowned at me, clearly unimpressed by my question. "Of course, Mommy. Why would she say no? Come on! We're all getting dessert!"

"I don't think so, young lady," I called after her. "You've had *way* too many sweets tonight."

Darcy just laughed and ran off to catch up

with Toby.

When I turned back, Logan was standing a step behind me, a hint of surprise and amusement in his eyes. "I had no idea," he said—but somehow, I doubted that.

I reached for his hand, and for a heartbeat, the world seemed to slip backward in time—to when I first came home to help my mom, to when Logan and I were still finding our way back to each other, before the years apart. Back when everything made perfect sense.

He lifted my hand and pressed a kiss to it, his fingers tightening around mine.

Bruno barked and bounded after Darcy, her laughter trailing behind like music. I smiled. In the end, maybe the best mysteries weren't about uncovering secrets at all—but about discovering each other.

To Be Continued...

I hope you enjoy the book. If you want to receive updates from future books, behind the scene happenings and

Montie Red

short puzzle mysteries, join The Detective's
Dispatch group here.

Click here if you want to check out more
books from Montie Red .

296

Acknowledgments

For your patience, support, belief in the cause, staying with me and tolerating the time that I took away from all of you to sit down and write. During these years, I learned so much from all of you. For listening to my stories, complaints, and successes. For your help and critiques, for all of these and more,

To Each one of you, who loves to read mysteries and took the time to read my take on them. My amazing coaches; Scarlett and Bryan, my mystery group friends, Mom, Gloria, Teddy, Josephine, and You up there...

Thank you.

About the Author

Hi, I'm Montie Red, and I have a not-so-secret addiction to crafting twists, turns, and mysteries best solved with a cup of tea (or maybe a snack). My *R-Parks Mysteries* series is inspired by my love for quirky small-town charm, meddling sleuths, and the occasional murder that needs unraveling—purely fictional ones, of course!

My biggest motivation is my amazing daughter, who keeps me inspired and grounded. We share our home with two lovable dogs, five chatty birds, and a husband who frequently attempts daring escapes from my writing world—usually by pretending there's a very important game to watch or a mandatory tee time.

When I'm not diving into cozy mysteries, I step through portals to other worlds, writing sci-fi and fantasy adventures under the pen name Monica Red. Whether it's catching a killer or navigating interstellar chaos, I'm always in the thick of an exciting tale.

Thanks for joining me on this storytelling journey. Grab a cozy blanket, dive into a book, and let's solve some mysteries together!